PENGUIN BOOKS

A STORY-TELLER'S WORLD

R.K. Narayan was born in Madras, South India, and educated there and at Maharaja's College in Mysore. His first novel *Swami and Friends* (1935) and its successor *The Bachelor of Arts* (1937) are both set in the enchanting fictional territory of Malgudi. Other 'Malgudi' novels are *The Dark Room* (1938), *The English Teacher* (1945), *Mr. Sampath* (1949), *The Financial Expert* (1952), *The Painter of Signs* (1977), *A Tiger for Malgudi* (1983), *The Talkative Man* (1986). His novel *The Guide* (1958) won him the National Prize of the Indian Literary Academy, India's highest literary honour. He was awarded in 1980 the A.C. Benson Medal by the Royal Society of Literature and in 1981 He was made an Honorary Member of the American Academy and Institute of Arts and Letters. He is at present a member of the Upper House (Rajya Sabha) of Indian Parliament. As well as five collections of short stories, *A Horse and Two Goats*, *An Astrologer's Day and Other Stories*, *Lawley Road*, *Under the Banyan Tree* and *Malgudi Days*, he has published a travel book, *The Emerald Route*, three collections of essays, *A Writer's Nightmare*, *Next Sunday* and *Reluctant Guru*, three books on the Indian epics, and a volume of memoirs, *My Days*.

*

Syd Harrex is Director of the Centre for Research in the New Literatures in English at the Flinders University of South Australia, Adelaide.

R.K. NARAYAN

A STORY-TELLER'S WORLD

With an Introduction by Syd Harrex

PENGUIN BOOKS

Penguin Books (India) Limited, 72-B Himalaya House, 23 Kasturba Gandhi Marg, New Delhi - 110 001, India
Penguin Books Ltd., 40 West 23rd Street, New York, N.Y. 10010. U.S.A.
Penguin Books Australia Ltd., Ringwood, Victoria, Australia
Penguin Books Canada Ltd., Ringwood, Victoria, Australia
Penguin Books Canada Ltd., 2801 John Street, Markham, Ontario, Canada L3R
Penguin Books (N.Z.) Ltd, 182-190 Wairau Road, Auckland 10, New Zealand
First published by Penguin Books India 1989

Reprinted 1989
Copyright © R.K. Narayan 1989,1990

Introduction copyright © Syd Harrex 1990

Page vii constitutes an extension of the copyright page.

Typeset by Tulika Print Communication Services, New Delhi.

Made and printed by Ananda Offset Private Ltd., Calcutta.

Contents

Acknowledgements

Some of these essays first appeared in *The Hindu* and were later reprinted in *Reluctant Guru* (Orient Paperbacks, 1974) and *Next Sunday* (Orient Paperbacks). 'After the Raj' was first published in *TV Guide*. ' Red-taping Culture', 'Family Doctor' and 'The Cat' first appeared in *Frontline*. 'The World of the Story-teller' is an abridged version of the Introduction to *Gods, Demons and Others* (Heinemann, 1965). 'The Introduction to *The Financial Expert*' is taken from the *Time Reading Programme* (Special edition of *The Financial Expert*, Time Inc., New York, 1966). 'Cruelty to Children' was Narayan's maiden speech in Parliament. 'Over a Mountain Range', 'Sringeri' and 'Kaidala' are taken from *Mysore* (1944). 'A Breach of Promise', 'The Magic Beard', 'Around a Temple', 'The Magic Cure' and 'The Image' first appeared in *Lawley Road* (1956) and 'Musical Commerce' first appeared in *Meanjin Quarterly*. Grateful acknowledgement is made to all these publishers and publications. The author and Syd Harrex would also like to thank Anne Harrex for her assistance in the preparation, in 1972, of the original manuscript of *A Story-teller's World*.

Introduction

While the literary items here have originated in the inquisitive mind and homely imagination of R.K. Narayan over his long writing life, the conception of this book too has a history bearing derivative traces of the metamorphoses and mellowing that attach to his distinguished literary career. The original plan for *A Story-teller's World* dates back to the earliest weeks of 1972, a Mysore New Year season of beautiful sun-swept days for which the city and its environs (Narayan's Malgudi) are renowned. I recall with paramount pleasure two visits at that time to Narayan's home where he graciously produced on the first occasion, for perusal and loan, a collage of some of his writings: out-of-print editions; unpublished manuscripts; a pile of magazine articles and newspaper clippings, the latter including a large number of his weekly essays from *The Hindu*. To be culled from this material was a selection of previously uncollected and neglected articles, essays, sketches and stories, and a year later—prepared and arranged in a form corresponding to the three sections in the present book—the manuscript was posted to Narayan from Adelaide, South Australia. It was promisingly entitled *A Story-teller's World*.

Owing to Narayan's contractual commitments to his overseas publishers as well as associated copyright obstacles, the collection was not published. He generously offered me publication rights in Australia only for all the material he had lent me, but that arrangement could not be proceeded with at the time. This occurred when he was one of the three or four major international authors who were the main attractions at the 1974 Adelaide Festival of Arts Writers' Week. The subject of Narayan's address, one of his abiding concerns, was the relationship between Fact and Fiction in his own work, and he illustrated it with a reading from his short story 'A Breath of Lucifer'. This is a theme which permeates the present book, a fascinating example being the 'Introduction to *The Financial Expert*'.

I remember, while Narayan was in Adelaide, that his polite rejoinders to routine queries sometimes culminated in an observation laced with his special kind of ironic wit and low-key chuckle, as when he remarked of our eminent Chief Justice and poet, John Bray, that he was both surprised and impressed by such an important busy man finding the time to attend the Writers' events, concluding 'he must have suspended hangings for the week.'

By 1974 R.K. Narayan was enjoying the recognition and fame he deserved as a writer who, in his irresistible novels of South Indian life, explored various manifestations of cross-cultural experience from the Indian (synonymous with Malgudian) point of view. (An example of this interest in *A Story-teller's World* is 'The Indian in America' which, as it were, complements the brilliant comedy-of-manners short story—'A Horse and Two Goats'—about the 'mutual mystification' of misunderstanding that overwhelms an American tourist's encounter with a Tamil peasant.) At the time of his March 1974 visit to Adelaide Narayan confided that he had recently commenced work on a new novel (*The Painter of Signs* published two years later),and he whimsically pondered the possibility that his then inchoate heroine could have obtained her sociology degree, feminism, and birth-control philosophy from The Flinders University of South Australia. Another fictional idea he entertained without transferring it from imagination to narrative concerned a hypothetical immigrant Indian family attempting to establish a farm in the Adelaide hills.

Although the *Story-teller's World* collection seemed to have dissolved into a state of oblivion that only optimists would call 'abeyance', it provided me with the raw material for an essay—'R.K. Narayan: Some Miscellaneous Writings'—which I wrote in lieu of the demisable book and which eventually appeared in *The Journal of Commonwealth Literature* (Vol. XIII, No. 1, August 1978). Most of the suppositions and views I expressed in that article preclude repetition here, but they may be taken to reflect most of the facets of Narayan's short works, as sampled in *A Story-teller's World*, which I find interesting as well as illuminatingly subordinate to his major achievements in fiction.

The contents of the original 1973 collection, moreover, did not suffer the fate of 'impartial annihilation' accorded to the 'review-cuttings, typescripts, galley-proofs, correspondence ... manuscripts' referred to in 'The Winged Ants' (an essay, paradoxically, which had earlier escaped its natural enemy—the subject of itself—long enough to be printed in *The Hindu* of 26 August 1956 and included in the first manuscript of *A Story-teller's World*.) Between a third and a half of the contents achieved metamorphosis in other collections: nineteen essays and sketches in *Reluctant Guru* (Orient Paperbacks, 1974), eight of which have recently reappeared in *A Writer's Nightmare* (Penguin, 1988) along with one other item (among the best of Narayan's autobiographical vignettes), 'Misguided "Guide"' which, like 'Reluctant Guru', was among the most appealing selections in the first *Story-teller's World*. Although the twenty pieces to which I have just referred were first selected for the original *Story-teller's World*, several have been omitted from the present volume because of their prior publication in book form.

The remainder of the contents of the book as first proposed in February 1973, however, has survived the devouring 'Winged Ants' of posterity for the time being—long enough at least to find their way here amid the following pages. To these the author and publisher have added some uncollected and recent essays ('After the Raj', 'The Indian in America', 'The Postcard', 'The Cat', 'Red-taping Culture', 'Family Doctor' and 'Cruelty to Children', Narayan's maiden speech as a Member of Parliament), while I have selected for inclusion three extracts ('Over a Mountain Range', 'Sringeri', 'Kaidala') from *Mysore* (second edition, 1944). This book, Narayan's first contribution to travel literature, is a rare, largely unknown, publication.

As I pointed out in my essay cited earlier, *Mysore* is 'an ingenuous blend of anecdote, travel guide, legend, history, fiction-writer's source-book and culture advertisements'. Writings in *A Story-teller's World* such as the *Mysore* extracts, 'Mysore City', 'The World of the Story-teller', and others, may be of special interest to readers of Narayan in so far as they reveal ways in which he replicates aspects of his local environment each time he re-invents Malgudi.

As the selections from *Mysore* indicate, it is a work that has probably served Narayan usefully as the equivalent of a writer's note-book. When 'Kaidala' is read in conjunction with 'The Image', for instance, we perceive that the first is an account of the famous Hoysala sculptor Jakanachari which, like a documentary, provides the basis of the fictional expansion of the legend in 'The Image' where Narayan employs the imaginative devices of characterization and dialogue to embody the theme of conflict between family attachment and artistic consummation.

In Narayan's short stories the narrative often focusses on a single central crisis or dilemma which may involve a specifically Indian issue or a universal problem, and usually entails an implied moral in the sense, perceptually, of something learned or understood. The narrative crisis may reflect a mode of thinking which is identifiably Indian, like the credulity of Thayi in 'The Magic Cure', or it may express a conflict like that in 'The Image' which is Hindu in context, with its emphasis on sublime dedication, while also presenting a parable of general relevance which transcends cultural boundaries.

So far as I am aware, five of the short stories included in this book—'A Breach of Promise', 'The Magic Beard', 'Around a Temple', 'The Magic Cure', and 'The Image'—have only been previously published in the rare first edition of *Lawley Road* (1956) and were omitted from the later, more widely circulated *Lawley Road and Other Stories* (Orient Paperbacks). In any case, most readers of Narayan are likely to be encountering these stories for the first time in *A Story-teller's World*. Moreover, they are exceptional among Narayan's short stories for not having been reprinted in subsequent different selections.

The notion of historical and metaphysical continuity, reflecting certain Hindu philosophical assumptions, is a fundamental value that pervades Narayan's *oeuvre*. It is both chronologically and symbolically enshrined in his vision of place, his ubiquitous Malgudi. Therefore, even the most dated of the author's early and minor pieces can have intrinsic period appeal by contributing to his comprehensive imaginative record of the human condition and social contract enacted in modern and traditional India. Narayan believes steadfastly in the literary doctrine of the writer as witness.

His short essays contributed to the Sunday editions of *The Hindu*, some of which are included in the middle section of the present book along with 'The Mirror' in the third, reflect the milieu of the early 1950s. In these cameos of journalism, and other generically similar essays, we have transparent forms of discursive discourse and comment; we encounter Narayan responding to daily matters in his immediate environment, or hypothesizing about 'global village' issues. More often than not, however, his non-fictional prose is most lively and rewarding when applied fiction techniques shape the writing, and when perspectives of humour mellow the author's opinions just as they irradiate most of his novels and short stories with the wisdom of comedy.

This seems to me an appropriate note on which to close this short Introduction, though I do so with a sense of ending that is a welcome rather than a farewell. Having enjoyed the personal satisfaction of introducing R.K. Narayan to successive generations of Australian University students, I am delighted on this occasion to perform, hopefully, the same role for international and, more importantly, Indian readers. If such indeed be the case, I hope to experience the sensation of a wheel of culture turning full circle. Somehow that appeals to me as a Narayan icon.

Adelaide   *Syd Harrex*
June 1989

THE FICTION-WRITER

The World of the Story-teller

He is part and parcel of the Indian village community, which is somewhat isolated from the mainstream of modern life. The nearest railway station is sixty miles away, to be reached by an occasional bus passing down the highway, which again may be an hour's marching distance from the village by a shortcut across the canal. Tucked away thus, the village consists of less than a hundred houses, scattered in six crisscross streets. The rice fields stretch away westward and merge into the wooded slopes of the mountains. Electricity is coming or has come to another village, only three miles away, and water is obtainable from a well open to the skies in the centre of the village. All day the men and women are active in the fields, digging, ploughing, transplanting, or harvesting. At seven o'clock (or in the afternoon if a man-eater is reported to be about) everyone is home.

Looking at them from outside, one may think that they lack the amenities of modern life; but actually they have no sense of missing much; on the contrary, they give an impression of living in a state of secret enchantment. The source of enchantment is the story-teller in their midst, a grand old man who seldom stirs from his ancestral home on the edge of the village, the orbit of his movements being the vegetable patch at the back and a few coconut palms in his front yard, except on some very special occasion calling for his priestly services in a village home. Sitting bolt upright, cross-legged on the cool, clay-washed floor of his house, he may be seen any afternoon poring over a ponderous volume in the Sanskrit language mounted on a wooden reading stand, or tilting towards the sunlight at the doorway some old palm-leaf manuscript. When people want a story, at the end of their day's labours in the fields, they silently assemble in front of his home, especially on evenings when the moon shines through the coconut palms.

On such occasions the story-teller will dress himself for the part by smearing sacred ash on his forehead and wrapping himself in a green shawl, while his helpers set up a framed picture of some god on a pedestal in the veranda, decorate it with jasmine garlands, and light incense to it.

After these preparations, when the story-teller enters to seat himself in front of the lamps, he looks imperious and in complete control of the situation. He begins the session with a prayer, prolonging it until the others join and the valleys echo with the chants, drowning the cry of jackals. Time was when he narrated his stories to the accompaniment of musical instruments but now he depends only on himself. 'The films have taken away all the fiddlers and crooners, who have no time nowadays to stand at the back of an old story-teller and fill his pauses with music,' he often comments. But he can never really be handicapped through the lack of an understudy or assistants, as he is completely self-reliant, knowing as he does by heart all the 24,000 stanzas of the *Ramayana*, the 100,000 stanzas of the *Mahabharata*, and the 18,000 stanzas of the *Bhagavata*. If he keeps a copy of the Sanskrit text open before him, it is more to demonstrate to his public that his narration is backed with authority.

The *pandit* (as he is called) is a very ancient man, continuing in his habits and deportment the traditions of a thousand years, never dressing himself in more than two pieces of cotton drapery. (But sometimes he may display an amazing knowledge of modern life, acquired through the perusal of a bundle of newspapers brought to him by the 'weekly' postman every Thursday afternoon.) When he shaves his head (only on days prescribed in the almanac), he leaves just a small tuft on the top, since the ancient scriptures, the *Shastras*, prescribe that a man should wear his hair no thicker than what could pass through the silver ring on his finger; and you may be sure he has on his finger a silver ring, because that is also prescribed in the *Shastras*. Every detail of his life is set for him by what the *Shastras* say; that is the reason why he finds it impossible to live in a modern town—to leave his home where his forefathers practiced unswervingly the codes set down in the *Shastras*. He bathes twice daily at the well, and prays thrice, facing east or west according to the hour of the day; chooses his food according to the rules in the almanac, fasts totally one day every fortnight, breaking his fast with greens boiled in salt water. The hours that he does not spend in contemplation or worship are all devoted to study.

His children could not, of course, accept his pattern of life and went their ways, seeking their livelihood in distant cities. He himself lives on the produce of his two acres and the coconut garden; and on the gifts that are brought him for story-telling—especially at the happy conclusion of a long series, or when God incarnates himself as a baby of this world or marries a goddess in the course of a story. He is completely at peace with himself and his surroundings. He has unquestioned faith in the validity of the *Vedas*, which he commenced learning when he was seven years old. It took him twelve years to master the intonation of the *Vedas*. He had also to acquire precise knowledge of Sanskrit grammar, syllabification, the meaning of words.

Even his family life is based on the authority of the *Vedas*, which have in them not only prayer and poetry, but also guidance in minor matters. For instance, whenever he finds his audience laughing too loudly and protract-edly at his humour, he instantly quotes an epigram to show that laughter should be dignified and refreshing rather than demonstrative. He will openly admonish those who are seen scratching their heads, and quote authority to say that if the skin itches it should be borne until one can retire into privacy and there employ the tip of a stag-horn, rather than fingernails, for the purpose. He has no doubt whatever that the *Vedas* were created out of the breath of God, and contain within them all that a man needs for his salvation at every level.

Even the legends and myths, as contained in the *Puranas*, of which there are eighteen major ones, are mere illustrations of the moral and spiritual truths enunciated in the *Vedas*. 'No one can understand the significance of any story in our mythology unless he is deeply versed in the *Vedas*,' the story-teller often declares. Everything is interrelated. Stories, scriptures, ethics, philosophy, grammar, astrology, astronomy, semantics, mysticism, and moral codes—each forms part and parcel of a total life and is indispensable for the attainment of a four-square understanding of existence. Literature is not a branch of study to be placed in a separate compartment, for the edification only of scholars, but a comprehensive and artistic medium of expression to benefit the literate and the illiterate alike. A true literary composition should appeal in an infinite variety of ways; any set of stanzas of the *Ramayana* could be set to music and sung, narrated with dialogue and action and treated as the finest drama, studied analyti-cally for an understanding of the subtleties of language and grammar, or distilled finely to yield esoteric truths.

The characters in the epics are prototypes and moulds in which humanity is cast, and remain valid for all time. Every story has implicit in it a philosophical or moral significance, and an underlining of the distinc-tion between good and evil. To the story-teller and his audience the tales are so many chronicles of personalities who inhabited this world at some remote time, and whose lives are worth understanding, and hence form part of human history rather than fiction. In every story, since goodness triumphs in the end, there is no tragedy in the Greek sense; the curtain never comes down *finally* on corpses strewn about the stage. The sufferings of the meek and the saintly are temporary, even as the triumph of the demon is; everyone knows this. Everything is bound to come out right in the end;

if not immediately, at least in a thousand or ten thousand years; if not in this world, at least in other worlds.

Over an enormous expanse of time and space events fall into proper perspective. There is suffering because of the need to work off certain consequences, arising from one's actions, in a series of births determined by the law of *karma*. The strong man of evil continues to be reckless until he is destroyed by the tempo of his own misdeeds. Evil has in it, buried subtly, the infallible seeds of its own destruction. And however frightening a demon might seem, his doom is implied in his own evil propensities— a profoundly happy and sustaining philosophy which unfailingly appeals to our people, who never question, 'How long, oh, how long, must we wait to see the downfall of evil?'

The events in Indian myths follow a calendar all their own, in which the reckoning is in thousands and tens of thousands of years, and actions range over several worlds, seen and unseen. Yet this immense measure of time and space does not add up to much when we view it against the larger time table of creation and dissolution. Brahma, the four-faced god and Creator of the Universe, who rests on a bed of lotus petals in a state of contemplation, and by mere willing creates everything, has his own measure of night and day. In his waking half-day he creates the Universe, which passes through four well-defined epochs called *yugas*.* Then Brahma falls asleep and there is a total dissolution of everything. Brahma sleeps for twelve hours, wakes up, and the business of creation begins all over again and lasts another full cycle of four epochs.

Brahma's own life span is a hundred celestial years** at the end of which he himself is dissolved, and nothing is left of creation or the creator. The sun and the stars are put out and the oceans rise in gigantic waves and close over the earth. Ultimately even the waters from this deluge evaporate and are gone. A tremendous stillness, darkness, and vacuity occur. Beyond

---

* Each *yuga* lasts for 3000 years, by celestial measurements; but one celestial year is the equivalent of 3600 years of human time, so that the four *yugas* cover a span of 43, 200, 000 mortal years. Each of the four *yugas*, *Krita*, *Treta*, *Dwapara*, and *Kali*, possesses special characteristics of good and evil. In *Kritayuga* righteousness prevails universally. In *Tretayuga* righteousness is reduced by one quarter, but sacrifices and ceremonies are given greater emphasis. Men act with certain material and other objectives while performing the rites, no longer doing them with a sense of duty. There is a gradual decrease in austerity. In *Dwaparayuga* righteousness is reduced by half. Some men study four *Vedas*, some three, others one, and others none. Ceremonies are multiplied as goodness declines, and diseases and calamities make their appearance. In *Kaliyuga* righteousness, virtue and goodness completely disappear. Rites and sacrifices are abandoned as mere superstitions. Anger, distress, hunger and fear prevail, and rulers behave like highwaymen, seizing power and riches in various ways.
** The equivalent of 311, 040, 000, 000 mortal years.

this cosmic upheaval stands a supreme God, who is untouched by time and change, and in whose reckoning creation and dissolution have occurred in the twinkling of the eye. He is the ultimate Godhead, called Narayana, Iswara, or Mahashakti. From this Timeless Being all activity, philosophy, scripture, stories, gods and demons, heroes and epochs emanate, and in Him everything terminates.

For certain purposes this Timeless Being descends to the practical plane in the form of a trinity of gods, Brahma, Vishnu, and Shiva, each of whom has his specific function. Brahma is the Creator, Vishnu is the Protector, and Shiva is the Destroyer, and all of them have important roles in mythological stories, along with a host of minor gods (whom Indra heads) and an even larger host of evil powers broadly termed demons—*asuras* and *rakshasas*; added to these are the kings and sages of this earth. The pressures exerted by these different types of beings on each other, and their complex relationships at different levels, create the incidents, and patterns of our stories.

The narratives may be taken to have come down to us mostly by word of mouth, at first, and were also recorded in the course of centuries. Each tale invariably starts off when an inquiring mind asks of an enlightened one a fundamental question. The substance of the story of the *Ramayana* was narrated by the sage Narada when Valmiki (who later composed the epic) asked, 'Who is a perfect man?' Narada had heard the story from Brahma, and Brahma heard it from the Great God himself at a divine council. And so each tale goes back and further back to an ultimate narrator, who had, perhaps, been an eye-witness to the events.* The report travels, like ripples expanding concentrically, until it reaches the story-teller in the village, by whom it is passed to the children at home, so that ninety per cent of the stories are known and appreciated and understood by every mortal in every home, whether literate or illiterate (the question does not arise).

Everyone knows what the hero achieves by God's grace, and also what the end of the demon is going to be. The tales have such inexhaustible vitality in them that people like to hear them narrated again and again, and no one has ever been known to remark in this country. 'Stop! I've heard that one before.' They are heard or read and pondered over again and again,

---

* Fixing the date of the *Ramayana*, the *Mahabharata*, or the *Puranas*—the source books of all legendary tales—involves one in calculations of geological rather than historical proportions. The *Vedas* are believed to have existed eternally—to have taken shape, as mentioned earlier, out of the breath of God; they had no beginning and will have no end. The antiquity of the *Puranas* may be judged from the fact of their being mentioned in the *Vedas*. A certain historian of Sanskrit literature fixes the date of *Mahabharata* at 3000 BC, and of the *Ramayana* earlier.

engendering in the listener an ever-deepening understanding of life, death, and destiny.

Most narratives begin in a poetic setting, generally a cool grove on the banks of a river or a forest retreat, in which are assembled sages at the end of a period of fruitful penance. A visitor comes from afar. After honouring the guest, the sages will ask, Where are you coming from? What was noteworthy at such-and-such a king's sacrifice? Tell us whatever may be worth hearing. And the visitor will begin his tale. Thus did Sauti, a wandering scholar, narrate the story of the *Mahabharata* at a forest retreat, when questioned by the sages. Sauti also mentions that Vyasa (the author of the *Mahabharata*) dictated the whole of it, his amanuensis being no less a personage than Ganesha, the elephant-faced god, who agreed to take down the story provided the author did not falter or pause in his narration. Vyasa accepted this condition and commenced dictating so fluently that the elephant god had to break off one of his ivory tusks and use it as a stylus for etching the text on a palm-leaf. Even today the image of the elephant god is represented as possessing only a vestige of a tusk on the right-hand side of his trunk.

All the tales have certain elements in common. Sages spend their lives in the forest, seeking a life of illumination through austerity and concentrated meditations (called *tapas*). Demoniacal creatures also undertake intense penance, acquire strange, unlimited powers, and harass mankind and godkind alike until a redeemer appears and puts them out. The demons Ravana and Taraka are such creatures.

The kings in the tales are men of action, waging war and expanding their empires, which is their legitimate public activity. The king rules his subjects strictly according to the code of conduct set for him in the *Shastras*. Sometimes he slips and goes through great tribulations (gambling is the weakness of the Pandavas, for instance). Sometimes the king goes out hunting, strays away from his companions, and steps right into a set of circumstances which prove a turning point in his life. Harishchandra is a good example.

Another common element in the tales is the *swayamwara* ceremony, the outstanding event in a palace, by which a princess, when she comes of age, can select a husband. Proclamations go out far and wide that the princess is about to choose her husband. Eligible princes arrive at the capital from all directions and fill the galleries in the assembly hall. At a given moment the princess appears in the middle of the hall, bearing a flower garland, looks about, and gives it to the one she finds acceptable. *Swayamwara* figures with some importance in the life of Draupadi, to take just one famous example.

While the evil-minded pursue power and the acquisition of riches, there are idealists who renounce everything, including the ego, in their search for an abiding reality. Renunciation is ever a desirable means of attaining a higher life, and at some stage every character of goodness adopts it.

Since didacticism was never shunned, every story has implicit in it a moral value, likened to the fragrance of a well-shaped flower.

Introduction to The Financial Expert

It is a general custom in our house for members of the family to sit around in the hall after dinner and exchange news of the day, talk of the town and general information before retiring to our respective bedrooms. At one such session some years ago my brother, who is a government official, said:

'Did I tell you of a peculiar problem we are facing in our office? We are unable to get rid of a man we have dismissed from service. He was a peon, a sort of head of the menial staff. His work was to look after the boss's desk, clear his trays, take away the files after the big man looked through them and distribute them to the concerned clerks, stand outside his door to keep off visitors, and allot the day's duties to the other peons in the office.

'We found in the course of time that this man was carrying on shady financial transactions among the staff. We have nearly a hundred employees in our office, and very few among them ever get more than a hundred rupees a month. Money is in short supply generally and is the greatest preoccupation, especially among the lower grade. We have established a sort of cooperative banking in order to help those in genuine need. This man I speak of involved himself in the transactions of this bank, and no one could get a single rupee out of it unless he purchased the goodwill of this odd character with the promise of a commission on the loan which might be finally sanctioned. The whole establishment stank with evil practices, thanks to this man, whom we nicknamed *Dhur Margayya*—'One Who Shows the Way to Evil'.

'We could not let him flourish in our establishment, and soon we dismissed him from service. He was taken aback at first, but he possessed an element of indestructibility deep within and found other ways to carry on his nefarious activities. Though dismissed, he arrived at the office punctually every day, but instead of entering the accustomed rooms, kept himself in the spacious veranda at the main entrance of the building, where we noticed him always in a conclave. We didn't think it a good sign, and so we served an order on him not to enter any part of our building. . . .'

Before I go on with Margayya's career, let me explain the financial background of most persons working in that office. As already mentioned, most people there suffered from a perennial shortage of cash. Not only was there the general rise in the cost of living; extra money was always needed for certain inevitable extravagances. The joint-family system (in which various members of a family live under the same roof, sharing the expenses if possible) places on its earning members certain inescapable burdens. Births, deaths, weddings and, above all, festivals, are budget-upsetting, as they always involve feasting and religious rites. Starting with two New Year days (according to solar and lunar almanacs) during March and April, and ending with Harvest Thanksgiving in mid-January, there are festivals celebrating the birth of a god, saint or redeemer, or welcoming a season, at an average of nearly two a month. I have not mentioned litigations over shared property or land, which could go on eternally, costing the parties, in stamps and lawyer fees, more than the actual worth of the property in dispute.

For all these, everybody needed extra money, which was traditionally provided by professional money-lenders, who were popularly viewed as well-wishers rather than evil genii. How else could one discharge one's religious or social responsibilities? The burden of indebtedness hardly ever seemed of any consequence to the borrower, since all that he cared for was the money when he wanted it. He signed (or more often put his thumb impression) on any paper put up to him. The important thing was the ease and speed of the transaction. Later, the money-lender haunted the office corridor in order to demand his monthly instalments on pay-day, and his client generally carried home a mulcted salary and made it up by incurring further debts. This system of living subjected a man to perpetually gnawing financial worries.

To change this outlook and wean the spendthrift from the money-lender, social reformers and government agencies set up cooperative banks to encourage the average man to save, invest and obtain loans at a low rate of interest when he was in real need. It was this item—the low interest—that attracted a man's attention most, but he found that the cooperative bank did not act swiftly enough when he needed money. Rules, regulations and all kinds of formalities delayed the progress of his loan application. Above all, form-filling often proved irksome as not all the constituents of the bank were literate. And so the average peon working in an office sought the help of a professional form-filler and then waited patiently for his application to move and fetch results. At this juncture the Financial Expert stepped in as a general helper and took charge of the situation.

Let me now revert to my brother's narration. The odd character, as he mentioned, operated from the veranda of the building without entering the actual offices. But soon the authorities threw him out of the veranda too. He moved to the outer gate and settled himself there. His stock-in-trade was a little box containing some sheets of paper, a pen and a bottle of ink. While he sat there, many a person came to him for the drafting of petitions and applications. As he was also well-versed in the rules and by-laws of the cooperative institution, he tendered advice and suggestions of practical value, charging a couple of annas for his services. He also had his own organization to keep himself provided with a good supply of the printed loan forms and other stationery of the cooperative bank, and he sold these for a fee.

His corner at the gate buzzed with activity. He encouraged people to borrow and spend, shattering once and for all the philosophy of thrift on which the cooperative movement was based. He charged his clients interest on small loans, and he charged for stationery and his service, including perhaps the wear and tear on his pen point. His customers cheerfully gave whatever he demanded, treating him as their invaluable guardian. This could not go on for ever; very soon the authorities came down on him at the gate. Next he established himself under a large spreading tree across the road. Again clients swarmed around him. He conducted his business more methodically now by maintaining a register of assets and liabilities of various persons known to him.

This was the character described by my brother, and we discussed him until midnight. Later, I went to my desk and wrote the first line of the story. That was on 30 January 1949, and the last line was written on 28 April 1950. As I went on writing day after day I found the character growing. It must be understood that at the right point fiction must depart on its own course, and soon I forgot the original. Then, when I was halfway through the book, a financial phenomenon occurred in our province. To mop up the post-war glut of money in various hands, a financial wizard arrived. He promised fantastic, dizzying scales of interest and dividends on the money entrusted to his care, and he became the only subject of conversation until he crashed and ended in jail. About this time the Margayya of my novel was maturing as a financial expert, and I found the new material just what I needed to blend into the story. So Margayya is actually a combination of two personalities.

Many things have changed in my country as well as in its miniature version, Malgudi, since the book was written. There are no longer 'peons' in government (a rather colonial label in India), but only 'Class Four Officers', who will not accept an arbitrary dismissal from service without questioning its validity in a court of law, and whose emoluments are nearly double what they were at the time I wrote this book. The peasant today enjoys greater prosperity, getting a better price for his produce, and also possesses a better sense of his rights, and it is unlikely he would place himself at the mercy of a man like Margayya. The banking laws have virtually eliminated the adventurer in the financial world and made it fairly safe for people to deposit their monies in any bank. The cooperative movement, though it is not free from internal strife and politics, offers agricultural loans and facilities to the peasants more methodically now.

Many years after finishing *The Financial Expert*, I finally set eyes on the original Margayya, pointed out to me by my brother. He was somewhat ragged now, as he sat on the bazaar pavement selling books. Apparently he sold prayer books, and calendar pictures depicting the gods, but to the favoured ones he produced from under cover a different category of books: nude picture albums and the *Kama Sutra* in simple language. His banking operation seemed to have crashed, and he had turned into a shady bookseller, very much like Margayya of the novel, who invested his last cash in a smutty manuscript. Here seemed to be an instance where actual life followed the pattern of fiction, and it rather confounded one's notions about fact and fiction and which arose first. One thing I may assure my readers of: since the original Margayya could not speak English, there was no chance that he could have copied his career from my book.

The Problem of the Indian Writer

I

All imaginative writing in India has had its origin in the *Ramayana* and the *Mahabharata*, the ten-thousand-year-old epics of India. An author picked up an incident or a character out of one or the other and created a new work with it, similar to Shakespeare's transmutation of Holinshed's *Chronicle* or Plutarch's *Lives*. Kalidasa's *Shakuntala* (fifth century AD), one of the world's masterpieces, was developed out of an incident in the *Mahabharata*. Apart from this type of work, many ancient writers dedicated their lives to the rewriting of the *Ramayana* or the *Mahabharata* according to their own genius. Tulasidas wrote the *Ramayana* in Hindi, Kamban in Tamil, and Kumaravyasa wrote the *Mahabharata* in Kannada. Each of these authors devoted his lifetime to the fulfilment of one supreme task, the stylus with which he wrote etching the stanzas on dry palm leaves hour after hour and day after day for thirty, forty or fifty years, before a book came into being. The completion of a literary work was marked by ceremony and social rejoicing. Economic or commercial considerations had no place in a writer's life, the little he needed coming to him through royal patronage or voluntary gifts. The work was read out to the public assembled in a temple hall or under the shade of a tree. Men, women and children listened to the reading with respectful attention for a few hours every evening. A literary work lived not so much through the number of copies scattered over the world as in the mind and memory of readers and their listeners, and passed on by word of mouth from generation to generation.

These traditions were modified by historical changes. Let us skip a great deal of intervening history and come down to British times. The English language brought with it not only a new type of literature but all the world's literature in translation. New forms such as the novel and short story came to be noticed, revealing not only new artistic possibilities for a writer but also stimulating a new social awareness. Our early stories dealt with impossible romance, melodrama and adventure on one side and on the other exposed the evils of certain social customs such as early marriage, the dowry system, suttee, and caste prejudices. Many of the realistic novels of this period are in effect attacks on the orthodoxies of the day. They suffered from didacticism, but there remained in them a residue of artistic quality, and many books of early Victorian years survive as novels and stories although their social criticisms are out of date.

Between then and now we might note a middle period when all that a writer could write about became inescapably political. There came a time when all the nation's energies were directed to the freeing of the country from foreign rule. Under this stress and preoccupation the mood of comedy, the sensitivity to atmosphere, the probing of psychological factors, the crisis in the individual soul and its resolution, and above all the detached observation, which constitute the stuff of growing fiction went into the background. It seemed to be more a time for polemics and tract-writing than for story-telling.

Since the attainment of Independence in 1947 this preoccupation has gone, and the writer can now pick his material out of the great events that are shaping before his eyes. Every writer now hopes to express, through his novels and stories, the way of life of the group of people with whose psychology and background he is most familiar, and he hopes it will not only appeal to his own circle but also to a larger audience outside.

The short story rather than the long novel has been the favourite medium of the fiction-writer in India, because, it seems to me: (1) the short story is the best-suited medium for the variegated material available in the country, (2) the writing of a short story takes less time.

A writer who has to complete a novel has to spend at least a year's labour on it. This complete surrender is something that he cannot afford, since most writers write only part-time while they have to be doing something else for a living. Fiction-writing as a full-time occupation has still to be recognized. For that what is primarily needed is a sound publishing organization. Before considering this, however, I have to mention one other factor—that is, the problem of language. The complexity arising from this can be better understood if we remember that there are fifteen languages in India in which writers are doing their jobs today in various regions. Every writer has to keep in mind his own regional language, the national language which is Hindi, the classical language Sanskrit (this is often called a 'dead language' but dead only as a mountain could be dead) and above all the English language which seems nearly inescapable. Some of the regional languages are understood only within limited boundaries and cannot provide more than few thousand (or even hundred) readers for a book. A really livelihood-giving sale for a writer can be obtained only on

an all-India basis. That being so, whatever may be the original language of
the writing, the urgent need is to have an organization, a sort of literary
clearing-house and translation service, which can give a writer a coun-
trywide audience. As conditions are, there is no general publishing in this
country. There are several publishing firms but they are only concerned
with the manufacture of school-texts, which alone, by diligent manoeuver-
ing, can give a publisher (and incidentally his author) a five-figure public.
It must also be admitted that on the other side all is not well with the public
either. A certain amount of public apathy for book-buying is depressingly
evident everywhere. An American publisher once asked me how many
copies of my *Bachelor of Arts* (in the Pocket Book series costing a rupee
and eight annas) sold in my own town (Mysore). I suggested two hundred
as a possible figure.

'What is the population of your town?' he asked.

'Over two-hundred-and-seventy-five-thousand.'

'How many among them can read a novel like yours?'

'At least five thousand,' I ventured.

'How many among them know you personally and like your work in
general?'

'Probably all of them and many more.'

'How many among them could afford to pay a rupee odd for your
book?'

'Perhaps all of them!'

'In that case what prevents five thousand copies being sold in your own
town rather than two hundred?'

I could not answer the question. I am still thinking it over. I think it is
for experts in the trade to discover a solution, and when that is done, a major
obstacle in the fiction-writer's way in India will have been removed.

II

In a well-ordered society there should be no problem at all for a writer. It
should be possible for a writer to dash off a book in six months and see it
automatically reach his reader, thus enabling him to enjoy a few months
of rest, holiday and reading so that he may begin a new book at the end of
it. How well should a society be ordered before this can happen? What are
the things that a dynamic reformer should undertake before he can create
congenial conditions in which fiction-writing may flourish?

The writer of a novel is afflicted with peculiar problems. For one thing,
the novel is a comparatively recent form in our country and though people
have taken to the reading of novels in order to while away their time it never
occurs to anyone to ask seriously who writes them. It never occurs to

anyone that no novel may be available for entertainment or instruction unless the author is kept in working order. What are the things necessary to keep this man in working condition? All sorts of amenities are devised in order to solve the difficulties of all kinds of workers. Even journaliṣts, hitherto the most neglected of men, have come to state their aims and demand their welfare conditions. But the novelist has as yet no code of social existence. The trouble is the novelist has not attained a vocal status.

The first problem of a novelist is that he must live without too many harassments and distractions. It is necessary that he should arrive at a sort of compromise between his inner life and outer life. A writer's life is a subjective one, and it may not always be feasible for him to discharge his duties competently as a captain steering the ship of family in the ocean of existence. Though he may be unexcelled as a writer of fiction, the facts, the hard-headed facts of life, may prove beyond his powers. I mean by hard and harsh facts such activities as balancing the budget, looking after dependents, calculating various things and so forth. He is likely to make grave errors of calculation when dealing with numbers, not because he does not know addition and subtraction but (his mind being all the time in the realm of fiction) because his cash in hand may appear exaggerated in value. He is likely to acquire the satisfaction warranted by the possession of 10,000 rupees when all that he has on hand is fifty rupees. This is rather a disproportionate way of dealing with figures but that is how he is and no one can help it. It is not a realistic manner of living and tackling the problems of life but what can he do, he is made that way, it is the only manner in which he can live and work. This creates peculiar difficulties for those who have to live along with him. However realistic a writer he may be he is likely to prove to be the most dreamy of persons on earth, and the demands of practical life may prove bewildering if not actually distressing to him, and against this he always needs something like a cushion between him and crude realities. I don't know what kind of organization could achieve this purpose but if something could be done to relieve him from the necessity of running a family, paying off bills, meeting creditors, and other such odious and devitalizing occupations, he will do his work in peace and the public may ultimately feel gratified that it has more books to read.

To understand this implication fully one must first have an idea of the method of his work. The novelist has to live close to life and keep himself open to its influence if he is to prove successful as a writer. His mind must pick out the material from life, shape it and use it. He is likely to be always busy planning the next chapter. Whether he is the type that sits down methodically to dash off a fixed quota of work each day, or whether he is the one to seize upon his work and go through it in a frenzy without a pause, the actual time of sitting down at one's desk can never be an indication of the quantity of work involved. Whatever may be the actual time spent at his desk, he is always busy. His mind is always at work. There is no such thing as finishing a piece of work for the day and rising from his seat with a free mind. There is no end to the work till the novel is completed, and if one remembers that a novel takes a minimum of 80,000 words, one may understand the labours involved. Many persons ask me whether I have in mind all the detail of a novel beforehand, whether I work out an outline, or how a novel comes into being at all. I wish I could answer that question with precision. I know one thing, when I sit down to write I have no more than a vague idea regarding the outcome of the day's work. It would be not far wrong if I said that my fingers on the typewriter probably know more about what is coming on than my head. It is perhaps no compliment to myself, but I do not intend it to be. The details of what I write each day, when I am at work on a novel, work themselves out. This means that one's subconscious self should have a lot of unimpaired freedom. Writing a novel is both a conscious and unconscious occupation; it is something both of the intellect and something superior to the intellect. That means the mind should be left completely free to continue to exercise itself at all levels. The intellect portion of it pertains mostly to technique and expression, and not to the ultimate shape of the thing, though there is always a possibility that the novelist has some idea of the shape of things to come, and to that extent his mind is burdened.

When he sits down on a certain day to begin a new novel, it must be understood that he is undertaking a task which will virtually chain him up for months to come. Even if he is a fast worker, apart from the actual writing it may bind him down for nearly two years. And then he has to spend a few months revising the manuscript, because it always seems to be incomplete and not quite satisfactory. Here revision means watching over 80,000 words and their punctuation, while trying to test the validity and worth of every word. I say nothing of the misgiving that may suddenly assail one about the sense of what one has been writing. It is always there and may involve the scrapping of months of work. Let us grant he has satisfactorily settled all the mechanical details of his work, and has parcelled off the manuscript to his publisher. This is his happiest day. He feels like a schoolboy who has written his last examination of the season, looks back with a shudder on his days of drudgery and looks forward to a happy summer vacation ahead. Now, how far can this author afford to keep away from writing after his two years of labour? If he is to be in a fit condition to give the world his best again, he must rest and recuperate while giving time for the springs of his inspiration to well up again. For that it must be possible for him to afford to rest: the work that he has done must reach the public and must be accepted by the public. When all is said and done it is only public support that can sustain an author. It is important that his work should appear in the bookstalls and that the public must show enthusiasm for it. This alone can help him to live by his best work. This alone can prevent his preoccupation with pot-boiling activities, whereby he pumps himself dry and goes on producing third-rate stuff when he ought to be resting. What exactly can give him this freedom? It is that state of society whereby the publishing activity is organized so well that a good book reaches its readers without delay. From this point of view the novelist in our country suffers greatly. As I've said earlier there is not a general publishing business here as in other countries. There are few publishers who are interested in publishing, advertising and getting the work of a new writer. For this cooperation from all is required, from the press which must make new books known through its literary columns, booksellers who must keep the book in stock, and more than anything else a responsive and appreciative public which buys the books. I use the word 'buy' deliberately. It certainly connotes a different activity from reading, which may be done with borrowed books. It may give an author a vast reading public without any relief or reward. A book-buying campaign must be started on a nation-wide scale. Buying books and building a home library must become a citizen's duty, which will have the double advantage of both rewarding the labours of the author and providing a general atmosphere of culture in every home.

English in India

When I was five years old I was initiated into the mysteries of letters with the appropriate religious ceremonies. I was taught to shape the first two letters of the alphabet with corn spread out on a tray, both in Sanskrit and Tamil. Sanskrit, because it was the classical language of India, Tamil because it was the language of the province in which I was born and my mother tongue. But in the classroom neither of these two languages was given any importance; they were assigned to the most helpless among the teachers, the *pandits* who were treated as a joke by the boys, since they taught only the 'second language', the first being English as ordained by Lord Macaulay when he introduced English education in India. English was taught by the best teacher in the school, if not by the ruling star of the institution, the headmaster himself. The English Primer itself looked differently styled from the other books in the school-bag with its strong binding and coloured illustrations, for those were days when educational material was imported and no one could dream of producing a school-book in India. The first lesson in the glossy Primer began 'A was an Apple Pie' (or was it just Apple, I don't remember); and went on to explain, 'B bit it' and 'C cut it'. The activities of B and C were understandable, but the opening line itself was mystifying. What was an Apple Pie? From B's and C's zestful application, we could guess that it had to do with some ordinary business of mankind, such as eating. But what was it that was being eaten? Among fruits we were familiar with the mango, banana, guava, pomegranate and grape, but not the apple (in our part of the country) much less an Apple Pie. To our eager questioning, the omniscient one, our English teacher, would just state, 'It must be some stuff similar to our *idli*, but prepared with apple.' This information was inadequate and one popped up to ask, 'What would it taste like? Sweet or sour?' The teacher's patience now being at an end, he would say, 'Don't be a nuisance, read your lessons,' a peremptory order which we obeyed by reciting like a litany 'A was an Apple Pie'. We were left free to guess, each according to his capacity, at the quality, shape, and details of the civilization portrayed in

our class-books. Other subjects were also taught in English. We brooded
over arithmetical problems in which John did a piece of work in half the
time that Sam took. . . if they laboured jointly, when would the work be
completed? We also wrestled with bushels of oats and wages paid in
pounds, shillings and pence, although the characters around us in actual
life called themselves Rama and Krishna and handled rupees and annas
rather than half-crowns and farthings. Thus we got used to getting along
splendidly with unknown quantities in our studies. At a later stage, we read
and enjoyed the best of English prose, overlooking detail in the process of
enjoying literature. Chaucer and Ben Jonson, Pope and Dryden, Boswell
and Goldsmith and a hundred others became almost our next door
neighbours. Through books alone we learnt to love the London of English
literature. I have a friend, an engineer, who happening to visit West
Germany on a technical mission, took off a fortnight in order to go to
England and see the literary landmarks. His literary map included not only
Keats's house at Hampstead, but also the amphibian world of the Thames
bargemen described in the stories of W.W. Jacobs; he tried to follow the
trails of Oliver Twist and David Copperfield, and also obtain, if possible,
a glimpse of the comfortable world of Soames Forsyte, nor could he
overlook the Drones Club mentioned by P.G. Wodehouse. He rounded off
the trip with a visit to Stratford-on-Avon and the Lake District, and
returned home feeling profoundly happy. Sometime ago a more scholarly
work appeared entitled *My English Pilgrimage* by Professor Sadhan
Kumar Ghose wherein one could find a methodical account of a devoted
scholar's travels in search of Literary England past and present.

In our home my father's library was crammed with Carlyle, Ruskin,
Walter Pater, and double-column editions of Wordsworth, Byron, Brown-
ing and Shakespeare. My father enjoyed reading Carlyle and Ruskin, and
persuaded me not to miss them. For his sake I read thirty pages of *The
French Revolution, Sartor Resartus*; and *Miscellaneous Essays*; twenty-
five pages of *Marius the Epicurean*; a hundred pages of Fielding and
Thackeray, and skipped through a dozen novels of Sir Walter Scott. We
also read many European and Greek classics in English translation. We
relied on *The Times Literary Supplement, Bookman, London Mercury,
Life and Letters,* and the book pages of the weekly journals, for our
knowledge of 'contemporary' literature. We enjoyed the literary gossip
generated in a society dominated by Shaw, Wells, and Chesterton. We
were aware of not only what they wrote or were about to write at any given
time, but also what they thought of each other and how much they earned
in royalties.

For an Indian classical training begins early in life. Epics, mythology and *Vedic* poetry (of Sanskrit origin and of tremendous antiquity) are narrated to everyone in childhood by the mother or the grandmother in a cosy corner of the house when the day's tasks are done and the lamps are lit. Later one reads them all through one's life with a fresh understanding at each stage. Our minds are trained to accept without surprise characters of godly or demoniac proportions with actions and reactions set in limitless worlds and progressing through an incalculable time-scale.

With the impact of modern literature we began to look at the gods, demons, sages, and kings of our mythology and epics, not as some remote concoctions but as types and symbols, possessing psychological validity even when seen against the contemporary background. When writing we attempted to compress the range of our observation and subject the particle to an intense scrutiny. Passing, inevitably, through phases of symbolic, didactic, or over-dramatic, writing, one arrived at the stage of valuing realism, psychological explorations, and technical virtuosity. The effort was interesting, but one had to differ from one's models in various ways. In an English novel, for instance, the theme of romance is based on a totally different conception of the man-woman relationship from ours. We believe that marriages are made in heaven and a bride and groom meet, not by accident or design, but by the decree of fate, the fitness for a match not to be gauged by letting them go through a period of courtship but by a study of their horoscopes; boy and girl meet and love after marriage rather than before. The Eternal Triangle, a standby for a western writer, is worthless as a theme for an Indian, our social circumstances not providing adequate facilities for the Eternal Triangle. We, however, seek excitement in our system of living known as the Joint Family, in which several members of a family live under the same roof. The strains and stresses of this kind of living on the individual, the general structure of a society emerging from it, and the complexities of the caste system, are inexhaustible subjects for us. And the hold of religion and the conception of the gods ingrained in us must necessarily find a place in any accurate portrayal of life. Nor can we overlook the rural life and its problems, eighty-five out of a hundred Indians being village folk.

English has proved that if a language has flexibility any experience can be communicated through it, even if it has to be paraphrased rather than conveyed, and even if the factual detail, as in the case of the Apple Pie, is only partially understood. In order not to lose the excellence of this medium a few writers in India took to writing in English, and produced a literature that was perhaps not first-rate; often the writing seemed imitative, halting, inept or an awkward translation of a vernacular rhetoric, mode, or idiom; but occasionally it was brilliant. We are still experimentalists. I may straightaway explain what we do not attempt to do. We are not attempting to write Anglo-Saxon English. The English language, through sheer resilience and mobility, is now undergoing a process of Indianization in the same manner as it adopted US citizenship over a century ago, with the difference that it is the major language there but here one of the fifteen. I cannot say whether this process of transmutation is to be viewed as an enrichment of the English language or a debasement of it. All that I am able to confirm, after nearly thirty years of writing, is that it has served my purpose admirably, of conveying unambiguously the thoughts and acts of a set of personalities, who flourish in a small town named Malgudi supposed to be located in a corner of South India.

English has been with us for over a century, but it has remained the language of the intelligentsia, less than ten per cent of the population understanding it. In view of this limitation our constitution provides for the changing over of the official language to Hindi in due course. Interestingly, side by side, special institutes are established where English teachers are trained, and the subject occupies a high place in all universities. I feel, however, that it must reach the market-place and the village green if it is to send down roots. In order to achieve this, the language must be taught in a simpler manner, through a basic vocabulary, simplified spelling, and explained and interpreted through the many spoken languages of India. When such a technique of propagation is perfected, we shall see English, whatever its official status, assimilated in the soil of India and growing again from it.

Toasted English

In American restaurants they call for 'toasted English', referring to English muffins which, though being made in America, now retain 'English' as a sort of concession to their origin. The same may be said of the Americans' language too. They too went through a phase of throwing out the British but retaining their language and letting it flourish on American soil: the resultant language is somewhat different from its British counterpart; it may be said to have gone through a process of toasting. One noticeable result of this toasting is that much of the formalism surrounding the use of English has been abandoned.

In America, they have freed the language from the stifling tyranny of the Passive Voice. Where we would say ceremoniously 'Trespassing Prohibited', their signboards, as I noticed in the parks of Berkeley, merely say 'Newly Planted, Don't Walk.' Or 'Absolutely No Parking' leaves no room for speculation, and no motorist need spend too much time peering out and studying the notice. In a similar situation our authorities are likely to plant a twenty-line inscription on the landscape to say 'Under Municipal Act so and so this area has been reserved, etc., etc., and any vehicle stationed thereon will be deemed to have contravened sub-section so and so of the Motor Vehicles Act, etc., etc.' I saw on many American office-doors just 'Do Not Enter'. The traffic signs at pedestrian crossings never mince words; they just say 'Go'; or 'Wait'. In a Hollywood studio I was rather startled to read, 'Mark Stevens—Keep Out.' Mark Stevens is a busy television personality who does not like to be disturbed by visitors. Incidentally it left me wondering why, if Mr Stevens did not like interruptions, he announced his name at all on the door! But it is one of the minor mysteries that make travel through that country so engrossing.

The 'toasting' of English has been achieved through other means also. Americans have evolved certain basic keywords which may be used anywhere, anyhow, words which have universal, multi-purpose use. I may make my point clear if I mention the example of the word 'check' which may safely be labelled the American National Expression. While the

British usage confines it to its bare dictionary definitions, the American uses it anywhere, this expression being so devised that one may blindly utter it and still find that it is appropriate for the occasion. 'I'll check' means 'I'll find out, investigate, examine, scrutinize, verify, or probe.' 'Your check' means your ticket, token or whatever you may have to produce. 'Check room' is where you leave your possession for a while. 'Check girl' is one who takes care of your coat, umbrella, or anything else you may leave in custody. 'Check in' and 'Check out' (at first I heard it as 'Chuck Out' and felt rather disturbed) refer to one's arrival in a hotel and departure therefrom. And there are scores of other incidental uses for the word. If you are ever hard up for a noun or a verb you may safely utter the word 'check' and feel confident that it will fit in. 'Fabulous' is another word that is used in that country freely, without much premeditation. Of course everyone knows what fabulous means, but American usage has enlarged its sense. I heard a lady in Wisconsin declare 'Oh, those cats of mine are fabulous'— meaning that they were eccentric. 'Oh, so and so, he is fabulous!' may mean anything from a sincere compliment to an insinuation that so and so displays a mild form of charming lunacy.

'O.K.' or okay is another well-known example. It is the easiest sound that ever emanated from the human vocal chords. Everyone knows how comprehensive its sense can be. 'Okay' is a self-sufficient word which needs no suffix to indicate any special respect for the listener; it can stand by itself without a 'Sir' to conclude the sentence. In this respect it is like 'Yeah' which seals off a sentence without further ado. 'Yes sir' or 'Yes, darling' are conceivable but 'Yeah sir', or 'Yeah darling,' is unthinkable. 'Yeah' is uttered in a short base-of-the-tongue grunt, which almost snaps any further continuation of a sentence. 'Yes' involves time as the sibilant could be prolonged.

The refinements of usage in countries where English has a bazaar status are worth a study. On a London bus you will never hear the conductor cry, 'Ticket, Ticket'. He approaches the passenger and says, 'Thank you', and on receiving the fare says again, 'Thank you, sir'. I found out that one could calculate the number of passengers in a bus by halving the total number of 'Thanks' heard. In any western country if a receptionist asks, 'Can I help you?' it really means, 'Have you any business here, if so state it.' Or it may mean 'Evidently you have wandered off into a wrong place, go away.' A man who wants to pass you always says 'Excuse me', while he may with all justice burst out, 'What do you mean by standing there gaping at the world while you block everybody's passage? Stand aside, man!' When you send your card in, the busy man's secretary appears and whispers in your ear, 'Would you like to wait?' Though the tone is one of consultation, you have really no choice in the matter. The thing to do is not to answer the question but say 'Thanks' and look for a comfortable seat in the waiting-room, although you may feel like saying, 'No I wouldn't like to wait. I have other things to do.'

The time has come for us to consider seriously the question of a Bharat brand of English. As I've said in my essay on 'English in India' so far English has had a comparatively confined existence in our country—chiefly in the halls of learning, justice, or administration. Now the time is ripe for it to come to the dusty street, market-place, and under the banyan tree. English must adopt the complexion of our life and assimilate its idiom. I am not suggesting here a mongrelization of the language. I am not recommending that we should go back to the days when we heard, particularly in the railways, 'Wer U goin', man?' Bharat English will respect the rule of law and maintain the dignity of grammar, but still have a *swadeshi* stamp about it unmistakably, like the Madras handloom check shirt or the Tirupati doll. How it can be achieved is a question for practical men to tackle.

The Indian in America

Said a critic: 'You sound noble in your references to America, but it is only smugness. Have you no judgement or are you suppressing your critical faculties deliberately? You talk of America as if it were the most perfect spot on earth where nothing can go wrong and all men are perfect and charming. How can one forget the America of Nixon-Kissinger, men who enjoyed the game of teasing our country in all possible ways? How can one overlook the unreasonable prejudice of the American administration against India simply because India was neutral? They were juvenile enough to try and bully us by sending their warships to our seas during our conflict with Pakistan.'

'I wouldn't bother about it at this distance of time. What you say was true at one time. But there have been changes. Nixon is out. Kissinger was in Delhi recently, and the whole country watched him, on television, smiling and friendly. I think it will be best to leave it there. One should not revive history blindly and stir up the bitterness of other days. It serves no purpose. Let us forget the past and see what we may do now.'

'Have you nothing to say about the nuclear exhibitionism that the US indulges in day in and day out without bothering how it might lead to a total annihilation of mankind? Have their scientists no sense of responsibility?'

'I don't believe in Doomsday. For every poison there must be a parallel antidote unknown to us at the moment, but will be known when needed. The same scientists may eventually discover a nuclear neutralizer which may save mankind. I take hope from our legends in which no demon ever succeeded in smashing up this planet though he acquired all the supernatural powers and became heady enough to attempt it. Something always neutralized him in the end, and the earth survived the tormentor.'

'Have you considered . . . how?'

'Oh stop, no more questions please, but listen. ∴. Don't forget I am only a fiction-writer and not a historian, philosopher, or social scientist. My habit is to take things as they come. Too much analysis proves a handicap to my understanding. Atmosphere, incidents and human types interest me most and I only focus attention on those aspects. It is essential that I should maintain my objectivity. I 'can draw conclusions only from a set of observed facts, mostly through a character study.'

*

I will now focus on an individual, a type increasingly becoming prominent, much talked about these days as a growing 'connector' between India and America. I mean the young man who goes out to the States for higher training or studies. He declares when leaving home 'I will be back as soon as I complete my course, maybe two years or more, but I'll surely come and work for our country—of course also help the family.' Excellent intentions, but it will not work that way. For, when he returns home full of dreams, plans and projects, he only finds hurdles wherever he tries for a job or tries to start an enterprise of his own. Form-filling, bureaucracy, caste and other restrictions, and a generally feudal style of functioning waste a lot of time for the young aspirant. He frets and fumes as days pass with nothing achieved, while he has been running about presenting or collecting his papers at various places. He is not used to this sort of treatment in America, where, he claims, he could walk into the office of the top man anywhere, address him by his first name and explain his purpose; when he attempts to visit a man of similar rank in India to discuss his plans, he finds he has no access to him, but has to meet only various subordinate officials in a hierarchical system.

Some years ago a biochemist returning from America with a lot of experience and bursting with proposals, was curtly told off by the big man when he pushed open his door and stepped in innocently. 'You should not come to me directly, send your papers through the proper channel,' growled the chief. Thereafter the young biochemist left India once and for all, having kept his retreat open with the help of a sympathetic professor at the American end. In this respect American democratic habits have rather spoilt our young men. They have no patience with the Indian tempo, while an Indian would accept the hurdles as inevitable *karma*. America-returned Indians expect special treatment, forgetting the fact that chancellors and top executives will see only other top executives and none less under any circumstances. Our administrative machinery is slow, tedious and feudal in its operation, probably still based on what they called the Tottenham Manual, the creation of a British administrator five decades ago.

One other reason for a young man's final retreat from India could also be attributed to the lack of openings for his particular training and qualification. A young engineer qualified in Robotics had to spend all his hours explaining what it meant to his prospective sponsors until he realized eventually that there could be no place for robots in an overcrowded country.

The Indian in America is a rather lonely being having lost his roots in one place and not grown them in the other. Few Indians in America make any attempt to integrate into American cultural or social life. Few visit an American home or a theatre or an opera, or try to understand the American psyche. An Indian's contact with the American is confined to his colleagues working along with him and to official or seminar luncheons. He may also mutter a 'Hello' across the hedge to an American neighbour while mowing his lawn. At all other times one never sees the other except by appointment, each family being boxed up in their homes securely behind locked doors.

After he has equipped his new home with the latest dish-washer, video, etc., with two cars in the garage and acquired all that others have he sits back with his family counting his blessings. Outwardly happy, secretly gnawed by some vague discontent, aware of some inner turbulence or vacuum, he cannot define which. All the comfort is physically satisfying, he has immense 'job satisfaction' and that is about all.

On weekends he drives his family fifty miles or more towards another Indian family to eat an Indian dinner, discuss Indian politics or tax problems (for doctors particularly this is a constant topic of conversation as a result of their being in the highest income bracket). There is monotony in this pattern of life, so mechanical and standardized. In this individual India has lost an intellectual or an expert; but it must not be forgotten that he has lost India too—and that is a more serious loss in a final reckoning.

The quality of life in India is different. In spite of all the deficiencies, irritations, lack of material comforts and amenities, and general confusions, Indian life builds up an inner strength. It does this through subtle inexplicable influences (through religion, family ties, and human relationships in general) let us call them psychic or spiritual 'inputs', to use a modern term, which cumulatively sustain and lend variety and richness to existence. Building imposing Indian temples in America, installing our gods therein and importing Indian priests to perform the *puja* and festivals, are only imitative of Indian existence and could have only a limited value. Social and religious assemblies at the temples (in America) might mitigate boredom but only temporarily. I have lived as a guest for extended periods in many Indian homes in America and have noticed the ennui that descends on a family when they are stuck at home.

Children growing up in America present a special problem. They have to develop themselves on a shallow foundation without a cultural basis either Indian or American. Such children are ignorant of India and lack the gentleness, courtesy and respect for parents, which is the basic training for a child in an Indian home, unlike the American upbringing whereby a child is left alone to discover for himself the right code of conduct. Aware of his child's ignorance of Indian life, the Indian parent tries to cram into the child's little head all possible information during an 'Excursion Fare' trip to the mother country.

In the final analysis America and India differ basically though it would be wonderful if they could complement each other's values. Indian philosophy lays stress on austerity and unencumbered, uncomplicated day-to-day living. On the other hand America's emphasis is on material acquisitions and the limitless pursuit of prosperity. From childhood an Indian is brought up on the notion that austerity and a contented life is good; also a certain other-worldliness is inculcated through the tales a grandmother narrates, in the discourses at the temple hall, and through moral books. The American temperament, on the contrary, is pragmatic. The American has a robust indifference to eternity. 'Visit the Church on a Sunday and listen to the sermon if you like but don't bother about the future,' he seems to say. He works hard and earnestly and acquires wealth, and enjoys life. He has no time to worry about the after-life, only taking care to draw up a proper will and trusting the funeral home around the corner to take care of the rest. The Indian who is not able to live on this basis wholeheartedly finds himself in a half-way house: he is unable to overcome inherited complexes while flourishing on American soil. One may hope that the next generation of Indians (American grown) will do better by accepting the American climate spontaneously or, in the alternative, by returning to India to live a different life.

After the Raj

'The Raj' by itself is meaningless. It could be a prefix or suffix to a proper name. You may say 'Raja' (king or ruler) or 'Rajya' (kingdom), in any Indian language. The Raj in its present form is a vacuous hybrid expression neither Indian nor British, although the O.E.D. (which is a sacred cow for us in India, while other dictionaries are useful, they are not necessarily revered as the O.E.D.), has admitted it for a definition.

The Raj concept seems to be just childish nonsense, indicating a glamorized, romanticized period piece, somewhat phoney. The Briton did not come to India for his health or to try on 'crown and jewel'. He came on serious business; empire building was no light job. It was tight-rope-walking all the time in a strange land, thousands of miles away from home; making chess moves against inscrutable aliens in a baffling culture. The feudal trappings were incidental to his mission, serving to create a show of authority among the natives. But the fiction-writer never bothered to write about the pioneers' trials, extracting from the subject only the elements of adventure and melodrama. So he wrote of shallow, but sometimes glittering men and women engaged only in love, fights, intrigues and adventures. It is the type of novelist who is in the news today, whose writings provide the stuff for million-dollar-TV and film entertainments, against a background supposed to represent India.

Even great writers such as Kipling and E.M. Forster, when they wrote about India, exhibited only a limited understanding, inevitable owing to their racial and other circumstances. The authentic comprehensive Indian theme if attempted at all will have to be pieced together laboriously, bit by bit, like a jigsaw puzzle, and even then one cannot claim to have obtained a total or final picture. India is too vast and varied in characteristics, types, outlook and cultural mores, though under a climate of common heritage. Any generalization about India must necessarily sound like the definition of the elephant in the fable, in which five blind men describe it according to the portion of the creature felt by each with his finger. Although I am an Indian and my stories have an Indian locale, I would not venture to generalize about the whole of India or about my countrymen living beyond my horizon which is South India. I feel more amused than angry when an English writer professes to present the picture of India or a *typical* Indian. Kipling's knowledge was confined to the barracks, mendicants in the bazaar, domestic servants, minor officials, sun-burnt bureaucrats and their memsahibs who retreated to hill stations in summer and during those temporary separations from the family (possibly) engaged themselves in minor sexual activities. Only this last aspect is likely to appeal to a film producer. E.M. Forster's *Passage to India* is the work of a writer who has honestly tried to understand this country and the people he met. Though limited in perspective its authenticity cannot be questioned. But this authenticity and the limitations thereof would not do for a multi-million-dollar project. To the film director changes seem inevitable. If one may believe his statements appearing in the press, a mere hint of a rape in the cave in Forster's novel is inadequate for a film treatment, it must be made explicit in some way; and then a heroine who is a prig and an inquisitive bore as in the original is an impossibility for the cinema: she must have feminine charm and appeal, and marry her man in the end. And so, Adela Quested is transformed into a charming victim of Indian contacts, who achieves her romantic aims finally, whatever might have been the author's plans for her.

I have myself suffered in the hands of a film producer on a similar issue. In my novel *The Guide*, the hero and the heroine part half-way through the story and never meet again. But in the film version she is brought back with much ado at the last moment to throw herself at the feet of the dying hero. 'We have paid the star three lakhs for her role and that's a lot of money. How can we let her get off midway? She will damn well stick till the end,' explained my director while mangling my story.

At one time the simpleton's view of India persisted in England. Cobras, the rope-trick, and *sadhus* lying on spikes were supposed to be the normal daily conditions of our existence. At Shropshire, which I once visited, an old lady asked, 'From India, sir? Tell me how do you carry on day to day with all those cobras crawling all around?' This was an extreme degree of ignorance but it was typical at one time. Most people in England, especially those living outside London, were unaware that India was no longer a colony. But now, the media's focus on Indian conditions has brought about much improvement in public knowledge. Also, the Festival of India held in London some years ago, extended over several months, has been very enlightening as many of my friends in England have told me.

History shows that India and Britain came close to each other for over a century, engaged (to quote an origin I forget) in an unholy wedlock, followed by a deadlock, and ending in a divorce. At first, the Briton set foot on Indian soil as a trader, established himself among the natives adroitly, consolidated his position through military force and intrigue, remote-controlled from England. Until the time of the Sepoy Revolt in 1857 the Indian attitude to Britain was one of acceptance. With the political awakening in India, the British maintained their authority through a velvet-glove, iron-hand technique. With the growing tempo of the demand for independence, the velvet lining wore out, and a phase of strife and suffering ensued in the country, culminating in Gandhi's categorical statement in 1942 that the only solution to the problem lay in the British quitting India unconditionally.

'Quit India' became a potent *mantra* inscribed on every wall of every city, town and village, and when people chanted the phrase the rulers lost their heads, prohibited by force the sound of it and erased the message from the walls with tar and brush, but it was ineffectual; the movement continued until a certain day in 1947, when the last contingent of British troops marched through the Gateway of India on their way out.

With all the irritants removed, a period of mutual goodwill began between the two countries. Britain was no longer an overlord but a friendly nation. Certain values of British culture and life were always valued but now the appreciation was redoubled. English language and literature continued to form an integral part of our education. Shakespeare and Shaw and Eliot are read with enjoyment. British publishers look for Indian writers, feeling encouraged by the growing interest in India in their country. My first novel in 1934 could find a British publisher only with much difficulty, and I think the publisher regretted it later, with not even a hundred copies selling. Today, my publisher feels encouraged to keep all my novels in print in a uniform edition. The British Council in major cities has established excellent libraries and from time to time also arranges to bring in lecturers, repertories and concerts for the edification of the Indian public. Oxford, Cambridge and the London School of Economics still attract young scholars with ambition. In sports, cricket which the British introduced less than a century ago is now deep-rooted and flourishing. Today, cricket tournaments are a national event. Even champions of the last century such as Hobbs, Sutcliff and Tate in England are cherished memories in India, along with their Indian counterparts of those days such as Ranjitsinhji, Pataudi, Nayudu, and Mankad. Contemporary cricket stars of England, Botham, Gower, Willis with their Indian counterparts, Kapil Dev, Gavaskar and Kirmani attract a crowd of millions when they play.

In the business world too, the Indo-British partnership is successful. A recent business report mentions that among the recent collaboration arrangements between Indian and foreign countries, the United Kingdom has sixty-three collaborations. The relationship between India and Britain continues to flourish.

SHORT ESSAYS

The Crowd

Any crowd interests me: I always feel that it is a thing that deserves precedence over any other engagement. I always tell myself that an engagement can wait, but not the crowd. It may disperse by the time I return that way again. And so I make it a point to drift directly towards any gathering that I may see on a roadside—often incurring the displeasure of my companions. But I am convinced that a good crowd is worth any sacrifice in the world. Seldom have I been disappointed: it always turns out to be something startling and instructive: a scorpion-gatherer on the pavement with his commodities; an inventor of toys who sells for eight annas a couple of dolls which execute an uncanny dance at the end of invisible strings; a quite unexpected array of books and journals; or a medicine seller who tries to establish his worth by performing breath-taking conjuring tricks with cowrie shells and Chinese Rings; or, I'm ashamed to confess—even a quarrel between two persons.

In a crowd a man can attain great calm—he can forget himself for a few hours. There are different types of crowds and you have to choose the kind most suited to your temperament. There is a kind of pleasure in frequenting the radio stand at the Marina; you get a somewhat different pleasure out of, say, passing through the Flower Bazaar Road at about six in the evening; or you may buy a platform ticket and take your seat on a bench at the Central Station platform till the last train departs: I know a person who spends his holiday evening thus and draws the finest enjoyment out of this occupation; or you may pass slowly along with your eyes open from Parry's Corner to Moore Market. During such a journey you have a chance to watch humanity as in a peep-show: in a dazzling variety and shape of colours, forms, voices, appeals and activities.

A slight abnormality comes over people in a crowd. They cease to be their usual selves. The shell which insulates an individual ordinarily is broken in a crowd: someone's affairs, whether he is holding up a medicine, or singing, or quarrelling with another, becomes everybody's concern. A quarrel is a private affair till a crowd forms, when it becomes state property and those who form the crowd set aside for the moment all their own occupations and thoughts and get absorbed in the central object, and try to view the problem before them with a judicious mind.

In a crowd how eager everyone is to spread a piece of information! You have only to ask: 'What is it all about?' and a dozen persons will be found thrusting themselves forward to give the information or again you may pitch your question to a man who hasn't known what has been going on but he will helpfully direct you to another who may be properly informed. There are many persons of this type in a crowd—people who are there just for its own sake, not bothering to know what it is all about. We have often known instances where one man keeps looking down a parapet on the roadside, and another comes up to find out what he is looking at, and another and another; and all of them stand there intently looking down the parapet. The question: 'What are you watching?' will receive the reply: 'I don't know, they were looking down and so I stopped . . .'

Our ancestors fully realized the value of a crowd. A temple festival, lasting over a week, is a unique opportunity for an entire mass of people to gather in a place. The fragrance of flowers, the cries of sweet-vendors, the colourful paper toys exhibited for sale; and above all the music of the piper reaching out to the largest mass of people with the simplest means possible, are all subtle ties, which bind hundreds of people together in a common experience.

The misanthrope who declares that he hates a crowd does not realize what he is missing in life. For human beings the greatest source of strength lies in each other's presence.

Our Dress

In almost all parts of the world we hear the common complaint that men dress in a monotonously uniform manner, but ours is one of the few countries to have risen above this limitation. One has only to pause for a moment at Round Tana or Broadway to realize what a wealth of pattern and colour this freedom has produced. Here is a man wearing a long-sleeved shirt, a vest-coat and a *dhoti* tied Bengali style; there goes another, as a contrast, wearing a natty *banian*, a green towel over his shoulder, and a *dhoti* in the straightforward Madras manner; at the bus-stand is someone in a three-piece suit, soft hat and complete with cane. If the observer's luck is good he may even detect a couple of flowing Rajput turbans of the colour of the evening sky. Or someone crowned with an inch-broad, coffee-coloured felt cap of other days. Where has this cap gone now? I think it was the first article to face annihilation when nationalism surged up in our hearts and the *khaddar* cap made its appearance. However, many people may still remember the early days when one went into a cap-shop, and keenly examined the lining of each cap for the imprint of 'X' & Co., London'. What a prized possession it used to be (in spite of its faint resemblance to the lid of a milk can). The man who wore this cap, along with a stiff collar, tie and vest-coat, was surely something of a fop in those days.

Now and then we hear talk of standardizing dress in India as if such a thing could be achieved by an edict. Considering all things our present system is perhaps the most sensible, leaving each man to put himself into any dress he chooses according to his taste and convenience. The busy office executive has no use for loose flowing garments. One belonging to the musical profession would sooner cut himself in two than get into a pair of trousers. The journalist or writer feels that a *khaddar* shirt, with a shining fountain-pen-clip peeping from below the third front button, is quite adequate for his needs. There are others who advance the claims of shirt and *angavastram* as the most graceful combination devised. You may be sure you will find an equal number to decry the upper cloth as a useless impediment (particularly if you have to struggle for space in a bus every day). There are inspired people ready to swear that they were the first to arrive at the combination of *dhoti* and shirt, with just a simple coat over it: they also believe that all mankind will ultimately adopt this dress.

The suit, like the English language, holds a very undefined position in our country. One can never be sure how far 'Quit India' should apply to it. Its champions claim for it manifold virtues—varying from the purely aesthetic to the purely utilitarian: it improves a man's appearance (if he has potentialities that way); it helps a man deliver (somehow) convincing sales talk to his prospective customers; and above all it entitles a man to be treated as a gentleman by fellow-beings. Those opposed to this system of dressing have quite a catalogue of its defects to offer, the chief one, which cannot be gainsaid, being that in wearing a suit a man acquires far too many things to look after: the time spent every morning polishing the shoes, pressing a tie, and covering the holes in the sock, and in getting in and out of all these, precludes any other engagement for mind or body.

Of course each man is free not only to dress as he pleases but also to press his own point of view unreservedly. Fortunately ours is a very tolerant country in such matters. There is also another virtue we possess. We are generally free from the tyranny of having to dress for the hour or for the occasion. Here and there, no doubt, we come across persons who rigorously classify their dress items and would sooner appear with soot over their faces than in a set of clothes supposedly of another hour. These are, however, a select group living in a rarefied atmosphere, the sort of people who would ask when invited to dinner, 'Indian style or?'—a very strange type of question, which has been possible only in this country. In this connection I cannot resist quoting a recent author: 'The Englishman who religiously sits down to his solitary dinner in a dress coat in the sweltering heat of equatorial Africa at least obeys an obscure impulse to safeguard his self-respect. The Indian who imitates this ritual from a muddled feeling that it is somehow necessary to his own self-respect is merely a figure of fun.'

Noise

This age will probably be known as the noisiest in human history. We create a lot of noise not only to show that we are in a happy, festive mood, to canvass votes, to advertise a commodity or a point of view, but also for its own sake. Noise is the greatest bane of modern life. Every moment of our existence we are being distracted by it, necessary noise, unnecessary noise, purposeful noise, and the purposeless, enough to fray our nerves and madden us. If the average Indian life is only twenty-six, we have only ourselves to blame for it. The noise in and around us is wearing us out at a terrific pace.

Someone noted recently that present-day babies are peculiarly loud throated. They look elegant and sweet, no doubt, but the moment they open their mouths they let out a shattering volume of sound. Schoolteachers do their best from the beginning by ordering every few seconds in the class-room, 'Silence, silence'. But it does not appear to have any effect on children. They remain the noisiest creatures on earth. I think there will be an all-round benefit if a period of absolute silence is introduced in every class time table with a prize at the end of the year for the softest spoken in the school.

Hawking in the streets has, of late, assumed dangerous proportions. It seems impossible to concentrate on any study or writing at home, particularly if one's window looks over a street. Even if one retires to the back of the house one may not be saved since the hawker seems to set the pitch of his voice on the basis that you should be searched out and pierced through and through even if you are hiding in the innermost recess of the house. At the moment I am writing this I see and hear two plantain-sellers coming on each other's heels, almost trying to bark each other out of existence. I fear that the Grow More Food campaign has brought in only more plantains since I notice two more hawkers coming in with the same commodity. Now for a variation, I suppose, a seeker of old paper and empty bottles is expressing his wish in a rich, space-filling baritone, a knife-grinder is employing an anguished cry like one caught in a trap, and many others follow in succession, all that we understand about them being that they are shouting something; it may be anything from gingelly-oil-cake to lotus flowers, brinjals or bangles. We are surrounded by a moving, vociferous market all the time.

I have a dread of living next to a man owning a motorcycle. When a motorcyclist starts out, the agitation he creates lasts half-an-hour, even after the machine itself has gone out of sight. On Sundays this enthusiast tests and touches up his engine, whereupon the whole locality is converted into a sort of gold factory. I say gold factory because, in my experience, it is the most deafening place on earth when the ore is pulverized before being treated with cyanide. This was all I could catch of the whole process when I visited a gold-mine some years ago. My guide was explaining everything to me in great detail, but I could only see his lips move, there was such a clatter all around. It has been the same experience for me in any factory. I have often been taken around many types of factories, but as my guides gesticulate and move their lips I give up all attempts at knowing how cotton or silk is converted into yarn and fabric. The noise of machinery is always at a higher *sruthi* than the voice of the guide, a fact which is generally overlooked by those who take people around factories. While all the explanation is going on, my mind keeps feasting on visions of a zone of silence.

I abandoned a very comfortable house once because of a neighbour who switched on his radio every morning at five, long before even the gates were unlocked in any radio station. The result of such an early switching-on was that the radio (the neighbour's) kept up a sort of humming, a most harassing accompaniment, unbroken like the humming of a thousand bees. I fear that this simile may mislead my readers by its poetic association, but far from it; this humming was like the skewering of one's brain by many instruments of torture, something like a pneumatic drill operating at one's temples. Why my neighbour should have queued up so early in the day in order to receive a radio programme was a thing I could never understand. Its only effect was to make me get up early since I did not like to lie in bed wallowing in uncharitable neighbourly thoughts the first thing in the day. Moreover I was not without hope since a friend who knows all about radios told me that my neighbour's habit of switching on the radio when the transmitter was still cold was the surest way of destroying the valves, if not the radio itself. . . . But nothing occurred along those happy lines, and I had to move on.

I sometimes feel that God, who constructed the human body with so much forethought and solicitude, seems to have become weary when he came to the ears, and left them as the most vulnerable portion of a human being. The result is that we spend all our hours hankering after something that we cannot attain, namely Silence.

Coffee

I never tire of writing about coffee. It seems to me an inexhaustible, monumental theme. I sometimes feel that it is a subject which may well occupy the space of a whole saga, if we may define a saga as a worthy theme expanded to a worthy length. I am planning a noble work running to two hundred thousand words, a mighty work, not the fiction with which my name is generally associated but an accurate and factual piece of work as solid as the table on which I am resting my hands now. The work will be called *A Study of Coffee*. The first part will describe the life and philosophy of Bababuden, a Muslim saint who brought coffee to India. He came from Mocha bringing with him a handful of seeds, and settled himself on the slopes of a mountain range in Kadur district, Mysore State. This range was later named after him, and anyone can see his tomb even today if he will undertake a short trip from Chickmagalur. The origin of coffee, thus, is saintly. It was not an empire-builder or a buccaneer who brought coffee to India, but a saint, one who knew what was good for humanity.

After this historical prelude I will go on to examine how far this vision of the saint has been fulfilled. This will take us into the intricacies of making coffee, a definition of good coffee, its colour, texture, and taste. Incidentally we may have to deal with the question of milk and milk supply, sugar production, etc. We shall have to study the different techniques of coffee-making, pause to consider what should be the right temperature of the water boiled for decoction, the actual fuel used for boiling the water, the hardness and quality of water, etc. There are persons with highly cultivated tastes who can at once declare whether the coffee they are consuming has had its water boiled over faggots, charcoal, or an electric heater, and whether the water has been taken from a river or a well. All factors that affect the ultimate quality of coffee will have to be examined, and then there should be a dispassionate assessment of the relative value of decoctions filtered through white drill, flannel, and metal percolators. What should be the precise meeting point of flavour and strength, aroma and taste, are questions that involve the higher aspects of the coffee habit. A few observations will be necessary on the question of coffee temperature. This section will be called Thermodynamics of Coffee. In this section we shall strive to decide the right temperature at which coffee may be sipped. It must be understood that the temperature has to vary according to the occasion; the hot cup you may demand at home may not be suitable when you have to gulp down a mouthful and run back to your seat in a train whose engine has just whistled and just started moving; and then the social classification of humanity—at one end of the scale those who sip coffee so hot that the tumbler cannot be held except by wrapping a towel round it, and at the other end those who demand iced coffee, which must be characterized as a spoilation of both good ice and coffee. I shall also attach a map of the country showing spots where 24 carat coffee is provided.

So far I have confidence that my outlook as well as writing will be pleasant, but when I come to write on the economic aspect of coffee, I fear I shall lose my equanimity. I fear my tone may become bitter. I shall demand to be told why coffee should be made so expensive as to make an ordinary consumer despair every time he goes to buy some. Is it the aim of the Coffee Board to make every coffee-drinking citizen a bankrupt? I shall ask how far we need an elaborate and costly propaganda machinery for a commodity which is too well-known. Why run elaborate coffee bars in order to demonstrate how to make and taste good coffee when the humblest amongst us can do it with a spoonful of powder if the mechanism of supply does not stand in our way? The fallacy of this organization will be fully explored and exploded in my book. Over-organization has a tendency to make simple things complicated. Don't we know that the betel leaf of which we can buy half-a-dozen for a copper can become rare as uranium if it is handed over to a betel leaf Propaganda and Marketing Board under the authority of some ministry? Such organizations have a habit of being preoccupied with the question of how to earn foreign currency rather than how to make our people happy.

There are one or two unforgettable remarks thrown in by persons in high places which seem to explain the present position of coffee supply. They say, in a heavily jocular manner or seriously (we cannot judge from news-reports), that people ought to drink less coffee. If they mean it they should wind up the propaganda machinery, and then issue an ordinance forbidding the drinking of coffee. As law abiding men we shall make a supreme effort to obey this order: we shall pray to Saint Bababuden to give us the necessary resoluteness to overcome the mad desire that seizes us first thing in the day and then give up coffee for ever.

Behind One Another

When our country was less civilized, persons who had gone abroad to acquire a Barristerhood or an Oxford degree, generally came back with a lot of contempt for our own people. It was a sign of refinement to display a distaste for what may be called the Indian Way of Life. They generally spoke of two things—noticed by them in London—with admiration. One was the unvarying good cheer of the London 'bobby' (the 'native' took time to grasp what it meant), and the other was the Londoner's habit of queueing up. 'Queueing up? What is that?' asked the innocent stay-at-home. The gentleman cleared his throat and explained at length what it meant, contrasting it with the habits of our own people.

It used to be quite a normal feature of our existence to struggle for a ticket, for any sort of ticket, whether for a journey or for an entertainment. I remember how years ago when cinema was a new art and they were trying to show the first Indian film at a Madras theatre we could not approach the ticket window for days and weeks. At last we took a wrestler along with us, a hefty man, who took a few paces back and charged into the crowd with a shout; he carried on his neck, tightly gripping it with his knees like a jockey, another medium-sized man, who pushed in the cash and took the tickets the moment they reached the window, while Samson's own arms were engaged in warding off the tide of humanity threatening to engulf him. He brought us our tickets but most of his clothes were gone and there were scratches all over him. Neither that man nor anyone else felt that there was anything unusual in it: the man who flourished his ticket wore the look of a winner. Our social conscience had not developed too much and we never thought that there was anything wrong in it—till the young barrister expressed his horror at it, comparing it with what they would have done in London under similar circumstances. From the way he spoke we felt ashamed of our country. All our heritage of philosophy, learning, art, the Taj Mahal, religious teachings, *Bhagavad-Gita*, temple towers, etc., seemed to mean nothing culturally; the absence of the queueing system branded us as barbarians.

Today there is enough of it in the world to gladden the heart of the most perfervid queue-champion. When the history of civilization pertaining to this period comes to be written, the queue-behaviour of the men of this age is certain to find a mention. The future historian will in all probability say, 'There are ample signs that people everywhere stood behind one another for hours and hours and the file stretched away for miles. Why they did it we will never understand, particularly as there seemed to have been plenty of space all around where they could have spread out. They seemed to have learnt the style from ants. The one behind took exactly the same number of steps as the one ahead, and if he stopped the other stopped. Why they did it we can never understand as we have no means of judging the inner stresses of those times. All that we are able to gather is that if a man's longevity was twenty-seven years, he spent a total of twenty years standing in various queues, at bus-stands, railway stations, ration depots, cloth-shops, cinema houses, and every kind of public place. Considering the time spent this way it is surprising how they managed to find the time to carry on their normal domestic or economic activities.'

When I project thus into the mind of a future historian I am doing a piece of wishful dreaming. I hope in the future queues will be unknown. It must be admitted that the queue is a necessity, but a cruel necessity. It is a sign of an abnormal, confused, and congested existence. Except for the young barrister of those days, no one likes a queue for its own sake. There is something comical in standing so close to another, watching the back of his ears for hours, with another person doing the same thing behind you. Even the most hardened person never likes to be seen standing in a queue. It is always recommended for others. Even your best friend looks away when he waits for his pair of *dhotis* at the controlled rate. It is no doubt a sign of self-discipline and social conscience to stand sandwiched between unknown persons, but secretly everyone tries to avoid it. Everyone hopes that he will be able to find someone else to do the standing for him. I read the other day of a Delhi refugee making a living as a stand-in at a bus-stop for *babus* in a hurry. Who knows how this will develop? It may become a specialized job, depending upon one's 'standing' endurance. Perhaps the understudy may employ sub-agents, organizing and controlling the whole business from his office table far away. It may perhaps become a new guild or the government may find it necessary to class it as an essential service. The possibilities seem infinite. With all that I hope the queue system will interest only antiquarians in the near future.

The Unseen Shop

There is the modern legend of a stranger to the city who stood at a bus-stand for hours scanning every bus-sign, finally asking a passer-by which bus would take him to the Black Market. We generally pretend to be amused at his plight, but secretly feel that we too should like to be told a little more about this black market. We should like to see what sort of super (or sub) men people it. It is no doubt a morbid attraction, like the instinct to peep into an operating theatre. We cannot help it. Our waking hours are too full of reminders of its existence. It is an all-pervading evil. It is so subtly constituted that it can hardly be seen. Elaborate government machinery is set up to track it down. An elaborate code of ethics has developed out of its presence: people are good or bad according to the colour of their transactions.

The common man may be forgiven if he, in his innocence, sometimes visualizes the black market as a paradise. He is sorely tried in many ways, and he may be allowed to exercise his fancy a little. The Black Market Puram is to this desperate soul a world of fulfilment. He visualizes it as a vast, well-stocked, though subterranean world, where narrow streets criss-cross, and muffled men move about stealthily like shadows, for they dare not show their faces. But how well-filled all the shops are! Here he finds everything from A to Z. A certain talcum powder which disappeared years ago can be had here in any quantity. It stays here in protest against government interference in regard to its price. Do you want that glucose, the lack of which took someone to the edge of the grave? Here it is, piled up to the ceiling. Foodstuffs, finery, clothes, motor cars (one never thought a huge thing like an automobile could be tucked away thus), black gram, and medicines. It is a world of bewildering assortment.

This stygian market, B.M. as it is affectionately known, is a monster left behind by the Second World War. Apart from its obvious evil effects, it is responsible for a certain pathological condition of mind. Because of its perceived presence, everyone is lusting to possess dozens of articles now. Everyone is constantly thinking of something that is not available. One never thought before that this particular carminative for the infant stomach or that brand of soap or that milk-food or tonic could become a matter of life and death. In other days, a man passed by these things indifferently. If somebody at home insisted upon it, he retorted 'As if we could not live without these things!' But now as he passes the shops he looks hungrily at the shop-windows, and if a display of any precious brand of stuff catches his eye he is ready to jump out of his tram or bus.

And there are those who make capital of this fixed devotion. They are again a type produced by the war. The magic sentence 'I know where to get it' is an Open Sesame for them in society. To a man of this type, the greatest pleasure is to have people running after him. Nothing is so pleasing to his ears as such words of despair from another as 'I don't know where to find such and such stuff'—whereupon he promptly comes forth with the assurance 'I can manage it.' He spices his assurance with a significant wink and smile. He likes to view himself as a saviour of his fellow men.

B.M. owes its birth to the War God but owes its continued flourishing condition to Red Tape. Taking an instance, though it may sound fantastic, a person urgently requires a little ginger for a *sradhha* at home. If it is a very strictly controlled commodity he will probably have to apply to the Director of Pungent Articles at Delhi in a prescribed form which is to be had on application. This Director may turn him over to the Regional Controller, who will probably intimate that it is not in his jurisdiction but in that of some other person, who may demand an attestation from the Registrar of Births and Deaths before he can agree to take any action in the matter. If the person is an ordinary man he will stand aghast at the orgy of paper-filling that confronts him, not to mention the amount of time and energy consumed in the task, and so when a cheerful soul comes round to say 'I can get you . . .' he just steps into the trap and keeps the cycle going.

It is a world disease. It has given a touch of absurdity to our very existence. I recently read in an English paper, 'Mr. A was fined £250 on each of four summons—two for conspiring to obtain and supply edible oil and eggs and two for obtaining oil and eggs without a permit.' And again, 'Mr. X, of Hampshire, was fined £100 for conspiracy with regard to eggs.' I saw in another paper a photograph of a society gentleman with a long broom in hand sweeping a public street—punishment awarded for black-marketing: a possible model for all countries: one should be forced to keep clean either the market or the market-place.

On Films

There was a time when films were disbelieved. Those were days when the magic lantern held its sway in darkened halls. A dusty beam of light falling on a patch of lime-washed wall, the voice of the lecturer coming through the darkness, explaining anatomy or travel, a baton waving before the static projection... You might or might not have grasped all the explanation emanating from the lecturer, but it easily held you in a spell.

Then we heard one day that a thing called 'bioscope' had arrived. We were told that pictures moved and gesticulated. It sounded like a cock-and-bull story at first. 'A moving picture! Don't you believe such things. It can't happen here,' argued the wiseacres till they saw it with their own eyes. The bioscope had arrived at a place called 'Electric Theatre' off the Harris Bridge. We travelled in a *jutka* one day to see the wonder. In the theatre we sat eagerly watching the screen in front of us. The hall darkened and figures appeared. We were shown a gentleman coming downstairs, picking up his hat and stick and walking out, a cobra swaying its hood, a lady opening her parasol and strutting in the sun, two boys jumping over a hurdle, and an automobile of that year's make coming towards us—this gave us the greatest thrill since the motor car seemed to come off the screen into the auditorium. People screamed in excitement at this part of the show. The lights were switched on, and we were asked to move out and make place for others waiting outside. This bioscope drew a lot of attention and became the talk of the town. People with an enquiring mind asked, 'How do they do it?'

At the next stage we were shown stories on the screen. A story ran into twenty-four parts, with six parts shown each week. A hero, a heroine, an important document constantly changing hands, and endless chasing and tormenting of the heroic set. The hero was not the unbuttoned-throat-rumpled-hair-love-lorn-crooning-type which Bombay films have popularized in recent times, but fulfilled the orthodox definition of a hero—fearless, strong, and noble. He knocked down his opponents with bare fists; he withstood an attack from a dozen persons at the same time; he underwent ever-multiplying crises for the sake of the document constantly slipping away into enemy hands and the heroine clung to him through every situation. Each instalment was shown for a week and cut off at a critical point where the heroine, bound hand and foot, was about to be pushed under a band-saw or an oncoming express train. As you anxiously watched the situation the picture faded out and a caption came on to say, 'Was Pauline crushed under the merciless wheels or did she escape? See in the next instalment at this theatre.' We bore the suspense and lulled our curiosity for a whole week and turned up at the same seat for the next instalment. No doubt the film was not yet very highly evolved: people walked about in a sort of jittery manner and a certain tremulousness was evident in all their movements, and most of the time we had to watch their lips and guess what they might be saying to each other. We thought it wonderful all the same. And then the big news came one day. 'They are showing Krishna Leela!' It seemed unbelievable. It was all very well to make a film in America, but to venture on it here, in this country! But the fact was there. We saw Krishna being born or Harischandra surviving his evil times.

The bulk of the population liked to see only our own tales and our own actors on the screen although the intelligentsia said 'Oh! I have never seen an Indian picture.' A cleavage occurred very early in life between the class which would see an Indian picture and that which would not see one. The film producer named the former his paying public and the latter intelligentsia. This word is very much in use in film-production circles. It means one who would see an 'English' picture rather than an Indian one, who sneers at the sight of gods on the screen, who has contempt for sword-fighting heroes in velvet costumes, and who constantly asks 'In which period have you set the story?' This man is obsessed with 'anachronisms'. 'What is an anachronism anyway?' asked a gentleman who had made a film of pre-*Ramayana* times. The man of the intelligentsia replied, 'You have shown a rattan easy chair in the *rishi's ashram*, with the young hero lounging in it. That is an anachronism.' 'Nonsense!' snapped back the gentleman, 'What is your proof that there were no easy chairs in those days? You probably think that we alone have the brains to make them. Anachronism! There is no such thing.'

*

The big news of this fortnight is the publication of the 'Film Enquiry Committee Report' which is a dry title. Instead they could have called it, 'What is right with Indian films and what is wrong?' The answer to the first question is, as discovered by the Committee, that India stands second in the world as a film producer, 275 pictures produced each year represents a capital of 400 millions, and 600 millions see the pictures every year. Nothing that concerns the film world can ever be in terms other than millions. It makes us proud that we have climbed on to the second seat in this world of million counts. But the satisfaction is purely quantitative and statistical. When the next part of the enquiry is taken up, 'What is wrong with our films?', many depressing facts come to light and we seem to be assigned the very last place in the world of motion pictures. On this aspect the Committee speaks with the tongue of the intelligentsia and concludes with a recommendation for the formation of a statutory body called the Film Council, 'Which will enforce standards of quality to make the film a purveyor of culture and an instrument for healthy entertainment.'

*

I had a friend once who was full of artistic theories and notions. He was exasperated by the aping and vacuity that he saw in most films. He said, 'The only way in which our films can be improved is to float a company and collect at least one crore of rupees.'

'And make pictures?'

'Oh! No. Buy up every picture produced as soon as it is available and put it out of sight. After all people make pictures only in order to make money. Our company will give back the capital plus the profit. One crore will be thrown away but it will save a very large public from cultivating a corrupt taste. We must have a nation-wide organization for buying up every picture produced in this country.'

Restaurants

Someone recently complained that the serving boy in a hotel dipped all his five fingers into a tumbler while fetching drinking water; this brought out the indignant repudiation from the manager, 'How could he have had all the five fingers in? It must have been only four. Otherwise he could not have carried the tumbler.' This seems to me typical of the utter divergence in outlook between two sections of the present-day population: those who visit hotels and those who run them. Probably in order to improve the situation a questionnaire was sent out sometime ago, intended to catch all aspects of the problem. I believe when the investigators attempted to elicit facts all that they got was complaints from the servers regarding work and wages, complaints from hotel-goers regarding quality, quantity, cost and everything. I think the committee gathered a voluminous quantity of paper, properly filled up. It is probably too early even to say what they will do with it.

Most people are miles away from their homes at tiffin time. This is a characteristic of urban life. Students, office-goers, businessmen, have no choice in the matter. It would be unthinkable for a man from Adyar working in First Line Beach to return home for his afternoon coffee; nor can he wait till the closing of his office. At office awaiting the tiffin-break is one of the pleasantest states of existence. When one returns to one's desk an hour later chewing a *beeda* one has definitely acquired a pleasanter outlook. Now, I would like to examine what has happened to the man between his leaving his office table and returning to it an hour later. No doubt when he returns our friend is chewing betel leaves and looking the picture of satisfaction but he has been through a trial.

He goes to his favourite hotel as fast as his feet can take him, but he cannot enter it. He has to wait, then push his way through a file of others moving in, and finally stand in a corner scanning the hall for a vacant seat. It is most awkward standing there, he has a feeling of waiting for a dole. His trained eye catches someone at a table sipping the last few ounces of coffee in his cup, and our friend knows that the other will presently get up.

He cleverly slips through the crowd and approaches the about-to-be vacated chair cautiously: he does not like to appear too inquisitive about the other man's movements lest it should look ungracious but hovers about the back of the chair with a look of unconcern while the man is enjoying the last drop. If the man at the table knows that his seat is wanted he will try to brave it for a while but will ultimately vacate it, unable to bear the silent, implacable pressure exerted by the one waiting behind him. If our friend is lucky—that is, if someone else more nimble-footed does not descend on the seat like a bolt from the blue—he can feel certain that he has won his seat. I don't think any election candidate could reflect with greater gratification on his triumph.

When our friend gets his hard won seat, what happens? He looks at the time. Half-an-hour wasted in manoeuvres alone. The sands of time are running low, he will have to be back soon at his office. He desperately tries to draw the attention of the man serving at his table as he catches glimpses of him here and there. At this point one is reminded of the epitaph for a restaurant waiter, 'God finally caught his eye.' Finally, when the server comes, his demeanour may be affable or sour according to his constitution; but it is patent that he is extremely harassed and fatigued. If he should run amok he would knock down all plates and cups and tiffins and tiffin-eaters as the greatest irritants in life.... But he asks formally, 'What do you want, sir?' And then the counter-question, 'What have you?' It is a routine question that a hundred others have already asked although the whole menu—Sweets, Savoury, and Today's Special—is chalked up on the board. The server mechanically repeats the catalogue of edibles at lightning speed, takes his order, and goes out of sight.

As our friend awaits the arrival of his food he notices that his table is littered with used cups and plates and remnants left by other people, and as he eyes them distastefully, a tremendous cry rings out, 'Table clean!', and a man arrives with a bucket overflowing with unwashed crockery and vessels, reaches over the shoulder of our friend, leaving him in acute suspense for the safety of his clothes, and clears the table: he then rubs the table-surface with a very damp blue cloth, which our friend would rather avoid looking at. There are a few other things which he attempts to ignore while he is in the process of appeasing his hunger. He tries not to look at the wash-basin right across his table which sprays around a vast quantity of water as person after person comes up to wash his hands, some of them none-too-gently. The general noise in this hall is something that frays his nerves—the radio (somehow our restaurants seem to have stations to tune in to at all the twenty-four hours), the deafening clatter of vessels dumped out for cleaning, somebody shouting orders to the kitchen, shouting across of the bill amount, customers greeting each other . . . through all this babble our friend can hardly make himself heard. He ignores the crack in the china cup which bears his coffee, and the notches and grease on the spoon given to him. He thinks these are minor terrors which ought to be borne patiently. When he carries his bill to the payment counter and the man there sticks it on a miniature harpoon on his table while sweeping the cash in, our friend is happy that he is out of all this trouble. Perhaps that's why he wears such a merry look coming out of a restaurant.

Glimpses of Thumbi

Morning to night his life is one of exploration, exploring the forbidden corners of the house, exploring the tops of tables by climbing chairs, and above all exploring the depths of your patience. It is this last which gives him the greatest thrill in life. He is ever trying to fathom out how far you will let him have his way. He climbs your chair and puts his fingers on your spectacles left on the table, and awaits with acute suspense your cry of protest: even his head is turned in your direction and his look is fixed on your face as his hand strays to those glasses. I am sure he would be vexed and disappointed if he did not draw from you that shout of protest: 'Hey, Thumbi, leave it alone . . .' When this object is achieved, he withdraws his hand swiftly, with a joyous light in his eyes. I have often wondered what pleasure it gives him to annoy his elders thus; but the answer to it is not so easily found. It takes a great deal more: a great amount of watchfulness and study and, perhaps, the sacrifices of one's glasses, fountain pens, and such other fragile possessions.

All his hours are devoted to keeping everyone around him astir. With the dawn he is up, and he is convinced that those around him had better be up too. To this end he lets out a cry at the top of his voice, walks on those sleeping, kicks them, and flings himself on them, till no one can stay a moment longer in bed. Thus starts his day. His first dangerous act for the day is to clutch the edge of the cauldron in which water is stored, raise himself up and peep in. After this he attempts to seize the fire in the oven. And then he shouts for his milk, but refuses to drink it when it is brought to him. On the other hand, he tries to gorge himself on raw rice, tamarind, and vegetable peel. He runs into the sun and stays there, though it is severe enough to dazzle and scorch all others who may go into the open. He prefers to spend his time out there when his elders are desperately anxious to retain him indoors, and insists on being indoors when they are eager he should play outside and leave them in peace. In the garden he constantly tastes the earth, though he made such a wry face over his milk.

Although he was so very ready to plunge into the deep cauldron the first thing in the morning, he fights tooth and nail now when his mother tries to give him a wash. He thinks a change of dress as unnecessary as a change of skin. And after the wash and change he attempts in a bound to get back to the garden dust, rather than to the kitchen where his mother wants to feed him. He resists wholeheartedly. But once he is in the kitchen, it is hard for others to get him out of it. He finishes his food but sits down again for it when he sees his father sit down, and eats with gusto as if for the first time, and then once again when he sees another, and another, till they chase him out and shut the kitchen door on him. There is another matter in which he is unable to oblige his elders with compliance. His elders think he ought not to rub his face against the dog's, but he sees no point in owning a dog unless you are going to hug his neck and lay your cheek on his cold nose. Not merely this: if a chance occurred, Thumbi would willingly lick the rice on the dog's plate. But his comradeship does not mean that he accepts the dog's view of how he should be handled. When Thumbi wishes the dog to follow him, he just pulls him along by either end—by tail or ear, and the squealing of the dog makes no impression on him.

This turbulent contrary life he lives till night; and he just falls asleep wherever sleep may overpower him. Or if he has no mind to sleep he will expect all others in the house to renounce their sleep too.

It is an existence which is contrary to all standards of human conduct; self-centred, autocratic, and as his father sometimes declares 'Only his height saves him,' which is a fact. For he is only half-a-yard high and has seen less than three birthdays. His name is Thumbi, which is just as well, for it conveys his daily movements better than any other word; Thumbi is that creature one sees in the garden lawn, gliding on transparent, fairy wings, flitting from flower to flower, sipping lightly the nectar of each, seeking satiety or permanence nowhere . . . This is exactly the attitude of this little man. Within the circumscribed limits of the home he is ever moving on light feet, and ever changing his course and object, drawing a delicious essence out of the hard facts of home life. He gives one the impression of being in a continuous whirl. Even moving in the same direction tires him and he is constantly tumbling and gyrating.

It is a wonder he is able to move about within the house. The outermost boundary he is allowed to reach is the garden path three steps below our veranda. And he has to confine his movements between the backyard and the garden. But the actual area is immaterial to him; the fellow seems to have a capacity to expand space. Such a conception might make our heads dizzy, but almost every moment of his waking hours he is doing it. It is but a few yards from the hall to that jasmine bush in the garden. But, for Thumbi, it is an infinite movement. You could hear the patter of his running feet for hours (by his reckoning) when he moves there, his fancy caught by a pebble or a piece of glass shining in the sun. And he never moves but runs. Space seems to unroll before him like an unending carpet. Even when we try to confine him to his room, he defeats our calculations by running up and down or in circles along the wall. It would be impossible to imprison this man. He defies all shackles and boundaries.

I suspect that he is considerably facilitated in his running about through fancying himself to be a motor car. His tongue is constantly agitated in imitating the hooting of a motor car, and his lips are tirelessly trilling in an effort to convey the sound of internal combustion. His most truculent moods can be brought to an end if the magic word 'Palani' is uttered. We were long mystified regarding the identity of this personality, but later discovered that it was the name of a motor driver who existed in the imagination of our old servant. When Thumbi is sent out on walks in the evenings under the care of the old servant he likes to run at top speed in the middle of the road, leaving the traffic to adjust itself; and our servant is too old to keep pace with him. Sheer necessity forced him to discover a way of quietening Thumbi and that he did by uttering the magic syllable 'Palani', one day. The mention of this name checked Thumbi's rioting, and he paused as if held in a spell. The servant described the grand car that Palani drove, the continuous hooting of his horn, and the way crowds scattered when his car approached. Palani might drop in suddenly any time and ask Thumbi to jump in, but he would expect Thumbi to be ready and dressed and on his best behaviour. Thumbi's happiest moments are when he is listening to tales of Palani or fancies himself to be Palani at the wheel.

This picture of Thumbi would be incomplete without a mention of his possessions. He has undisputed mastery over an old rattan-box which once upon a time served as a tiffin-set container. It is without its lid, and this suits Thumbi's purpose better. He flings into it whatever he likes to keep. When he wants a thing out of it, he holds the box upside down. At such times we get a colourful, dazzling glimpse of its contents: a green tin engine without springs or wheels, odd coloured blocks of wood, a whistle with the mouthpiece chewed off, a piece of glass, a battered cardboard box, and a hefty wooden elephant without wheels but other parts intact. His box presents an appearance of wreckage for the simple reason that he subjects every article given to him to gruelling tests and attempts to resolve it into its component parts. Few articles ever survive the ordeal, the elephant being the sole exception. These are the only terms on which he is prepared to accept and retain gifts. It does not mean that he does not like them. Sometimes when he is silent and out of sight you may be sure of finding him with his face buried in his box; or sitting in a corner with his back to the world, lost in the intricacies of his wheel-less engine.

He has his own view of human beings. In order of importance: mother, father and others. To him the greatest abiding reality is mother. She is very good. One can do what one pleases with her. She is always there answering whenever called day or night ('Mothers don't sleep' he thinks for a long time). Father is slightly different. He is constantly out of home, when he returns he fondles much, no doubt, but his voice sometimes grates on one's ears. He has a tendency to shout and frown when anything goes wrong. The rest of mankind is all the same for Thumbi. They all loom over him, pinch his cheeks, lift him up, put him down, and give him sweets. Pleasant people, Thumbi thinks. However, if he is asked to pick out anyone from the vast crowded world he would choose the old servant—a man worthy of respect and love. Thumbi respects him for his friendship with that great personality Palani, and loves him because he never expects Thumbi to do any of the things his father and mother ask him to do. More than anything else the servant, being an unlettered simple creature, has the capacity to 'enter that world as a little child.'

Thumbi's Schooling

It is fascinating to watch Thumbi when he goes to school every morning. He is incredibly small; hardly a couple of feet in height, and unnoticeable when he is walking on the road under the sky. He wears a long sleeved shirt and pyjamas, and looks a miniature man, as he slings his yellow carpet-bag over his shoulder and walks along the edge of the road. He insists that the servant sent as his escort should follow at a distance in order to give him a feeling of going all by himself. His classes begin at 8.30 a.m. but you will find him on the road even at 9.15. Time does not bother him very much. All kinds of things attract his attention and hinder his progress. He watches with a thrill every minute leaf or feather fluttering on the road and stops to pick up any shining object lying there. One day a chameleon darting across the road made him let out a yell of joy of recognition, 'Oh, our lizard is going somewhere.' 'How do you know it is our lizard?' asked the servant. 'I know,' Thumbi replied peremptorily. 'It lives in that mango tree in our house.' And then he sat down to watch the ditch into which it had disappeared. He sat there for a long time hoping that it would come out, refusing to get up till the servant pretended to see it farther off: 'Let us get up and go, the lizard seems to be going ahead of us to school.'

At school, Thumbi has his own law. The servant should stop at the gate and turn back. From the gate Thumbi sets up a fast run to the steps of the main building, for he must reach it before the 'old woman' spots him; he feels he is done for if seen by her at the gate. If she sees him, she obstructs his way to the main building, snatches his bag from his hand, takes him up in her arms, and carries him off to the Toddlers' Section. Thumbi doesn't care for the Toddlers' Section, where a score of children like him are gathered, learning the alphabet, singing, and tumbling over one another. It is an attractive place, full of charts, and cubes, and playthings. Children take to this chamber very kindly and it is usually difficult to get them out of it at the end of a day. But with Thumbi it is different. Somehow he has an aversion to this place. If he is unfortunate enough to be carried away there, he seizes the first opportunity to slip out and make a dash for the main hall. There he has a sense of security in a senior class, where his sister studies. He quietly goes and sits behind her, takes his slate out and methodically keeps scratching on it, while the teacher is talking to the class. Nobody can be quieter than he when he sits there. He knows he is there on sufferance. If he is bored, he just goes and rides the rocking horse, or drags the bear on wheels (these are kept in a corner of the school hall). Nobody objects to anything he does there, for it is definitely recognized that it is good enough if he stays in the school at all.

On the first day he went to school, he started out very enthusiastically no doubt, but he was under a misapprehension that his father would also keep him company throughout. When he understood that his father was not going to educate himself, he lost interest and every morning devised a fresh excuse to stay at home. According to him it was raining hard at school; there was a tiger prowling about the place; fearful men attempted to waylay school-goers; the teachers had told them not to come to school; and so on.

Thumbi's schooling began rather abruptly. It could not be said that his parents had conceived a desire to see him better cultivated and informed all of a sudden, for, seeing his size, no one could associate him with school. But he brought it on himself. Nature had endowed him with an outlook where restrictions were neither felt nor recognized. There was little gap between thought and realization. Impulse was action; desire was possession. He didn't feel called upon to follow the dictates of anyone higher than his inner self. And his inner self said: 'Why don't you tip off that bowl of milk on that table' or 'Snatch the toy that girl is holding; if possible, also give her a slap on the cheek.' Thumbi followed these dictates implicitly. The result was, in a home of many adults and many children—anarchy. The only authority he respected at home was his father, but that good man had to be away at the office ten hours a day. In the evening as soon as his father returned many voices poured into his ears tales of Thumbi's lawlessness for the day. His father, if he had had a bad day at the office, pinched him or slapped his back and growled at him. Or if he was in a good mood he took him out for a walk and preached to him on the way, saying 'Thumbi you must not' and 'You must . . .' very earnestly, to all of which Thumbi answered: 'A parrot came to our house today, father.' Matters came to a head one evening when his father came home from office and heard sensational accounts of Thumbi's activities. He had called the servant maid names (vile words he had picked up from a gardener in the next house), struck a match and reduced to ash a celluloid comb, refused to drink milk unless fed out of a bottle like an infant, and above all kicked the football once again at his grandmother and broken her spectacles.

Father proclaimed: 'Thumbi, you are going to school tomorrow.'

'Why?' Thumbi asked, calmly sitting on his tricycle. He was lectured to. Thumbi muttered some reply in a very off-hand manner because he was very much absorbed in watching a bee droning at the rafters. When it was all over, he just asked, 'Are you taking me out for a walk today? I will be good.' His father was in a bad mood. 'Rascal, I will send you to school tomorrow. That's settled,' he said.

'Will you buy me a bag like the one sister has? I won't go to school unless you buy me a bag.'

'Yes.'

'Buy me also a pencil and slate; otherwise I won't go to school,' Thumbi said. When his father promised to get him these, he let out a shriek of joy. 'I will thrash you, if you don't go to school regularly after all this,' his father swore.

The next morning they woke him up. His mother gave him his milk, combed his hair, washed his face and thrust him into new pyjamas and shirt. He slung his yellow carpet-bag across his shoulder and walked out. His mother somehow felt saddened by this spectacle and followed him to the gate. His grandmother stood at the doorway and mumbled: 'Be a nice boy, too young, however, to be put to school.' Thumbi's father glared at her and marched him off, with a determined look. Going down the road, they were a grotesque pair; Thumbi looking absurdly small, hardly coming up to the knees of his escort. He was continuously remarking on all the surrounding objects and his father felt a sudden pity for him and said, 'Give me the bag, I will carry it.' 'No,' Thumbi said, 'They will be angry in our school if I don't take the bag.'

It began thus. Now Thumbi goes to school every morning. He rises early, picks up his bag and thrusts into it his slate and anything else that may be near at hand. He is constantly talking of what they are saying and doing in his class; the stories his teacher narrates and the grimaces his friends make; but all that, if accurate, must refer to his sister's class: he never for a moment brooks the suggestion that he belongs elsewhere. He is full of memories of his class and constantly checks himself with, 'The teacher will be angry if I don't . . .' Sometimes he says: 'My teacher has asked me to bring new books today,' and he picks up any old diary or catalogue or magazine and stuffs it into his bag. On the whole he is very proud and happy about his school and is very regular in attendance, refusing to stay at home even on holidays. Seeing him so satisfied about it, his father sometimes feels disturbed. He realizes that at least one good weapon in his armoury has been removed—he can no longer threaten Thumbi with school for unwholesome conduct.

The Election Game

The fever of elections which seized the city during the first half of this month has noticeably subsided. The posters on the walls are already discolouring and peeling away. The loudspeakers have been packed and stored away. Slogan-shouters and lecturers are recuperating in silence and whispers. Superannuated automobiles which had been kicked into temporary activity as beasts of burden to carry loudspeakers, placards, demonstrators and what-not, have limped back to their workshops. A lassitude has come over the city, similar to the feeling one experiences on the day after the fair. The meeting places where thousands gathered every evening and where thundering speeches were heard are deserted and the normal lounging by the local cows has resumed there. Now the interest of the public is all in watching the results to know who has gone up by thousands and who is going down by hundreds. People are becoming aware of the subtleties of the English language; everyone discusses the difference between 'unseated' and 'defeated'.

Viewed as a large-scale rehearsal for political life, I feel, apart from other considerations, this election has been a great success. When the principle of adult franchise was adopted, there were many doubts whether it would be practicable in a country like ours, where only three or four out of a hundred could spell their way through an election manifesto. But it looks as though they have got over this difficulty by not depending too much on the written word but on the spoken, or rather the shouted word; and irrespective of whether a particular candidate has won or lost or spoken sense or nonsense, the activity itself has been a success if it is viewed as a means of political education. Now even persons whom one would not normally associate with a sense of authority discuss (as they halt for a moment in *paan* shops or bus-stands) whom they will have the country ruled by and whom they will not. It seems as though a sense of sovereignty has been roused even in the most insignificant of us.

One notices that children too have adopted electioneering as one of their games. I know of at least one fellow called Ramu whose house was in the proximity of an election-meetings ground. It was great entertainment for him while it lasted. He used to be the first to arrive and take his seat even when the dais was just being put up. He studied in a school nearby but his mind was far away from his studies. When events of tremendous conse- quence were convulsing the country, it was not the occasion to talk about the Gulf Stream or the Great Mughals or speculate what would happen if a number of persons could do a piece of work in a certain number of days. He had put away his notebooks and homework, with the intention of taking them up again the moment the country settled into its normal routine. He went about the house always mumbling 'vote for this' or 'vote for that …' echoing all the slogans he had been hearing all day in the streets. When he went over to the next house to meet his friends he plunged into a game of demonstrations and counter-demonstrations. On the eve of voting Ramu and his friends spent long hours not only in vigorous demonstrations but also in excited discussions.

'My father has promised to take me too for voting,' said one.

'Nonsense. We won't be allowed to go there; it is only for grown-ups.'

'You are young. It seems anyone can vote, didn't you hear what they said in the meetings?'

'Not everybody, only tall persons will be allowed to vote.'

'No. It is all wrong. What about our geography master? He is our height and I know he is going to vote.'

'What is a vote like?'

'My father said it is made of paper.'

'What is its shape?'

'We are not allowed to see it.'

'I am going to slip in somehow and see what it is like. They are going to have it after all in our school. . . .'

'You will be handcuffed if you go there, it is against the law to try and see a vote. Don't you see how many police they have kept there?'

'I don't care if the police take me. I am going to get in there and shout "vote for Mango Mark".'

'Why Mango?'

'Because I like mangoes.'

'I will go and outshout you there. I will cry "vote for x".'

'Why x?'

'It seems when he becomes a minister he will abolish arithmetic and make cricket compulsory.'

Needless to say when the elders went out to cast their votes, they left the children behind much to their chagrin, which increased when the elders came back and displayed the little dot on their fingers. It made a little girl called Kamala very jealous, and she vowed, 'See if I don't get my vote very soon. And when they put that dot on I will tell them to place it between my eyebrows. . .'

Rice and Hospitality

After years of rationing, once again we see rice on the pavement, sold like any other commodity. For the first time these many years the rice dealer is willing to exhibit his stock and solicit custom. Apart from other benefits this will probably mean the reinstatement of the virtue of hospitality in our homes. In those days of juggling with fractions of-ounces on ration-cards, when a guest arrived, one's first thought was, 'Oh, God! How shall I provide the calories for this man?'—a most demoralizing line of thought. The depth of degradation was reached when one was obliged to print on marriage invitations the legend 'Please bring your rations along.' Of course no one would take it literally but if a food inspector suddenly burst upon a group of diners he would see that the food regulations were being honoured—just a party of thirty consuming their own rations, while the wedding host provided them only a place to spread their leaves about. It was sometimes feared that an over-zealous inspector might check the number of leaves thrown into the garbage bin. I don't think food auditing was pushed to that extent but it must be admitted that the host in a marriage party always felt nervous and advised his helpers to remember to bury the dined-off leaves deep and out of sight. And then the manner of inviting guests to rise for dinner was itself conducted with an air of intrigue. While the music went on, the host went round and unobtrusively whispered in the ears of his guests of honour: 'Get up, will you.' The guests would leave their seats without a word, and with the air of men assisting in an assassination, vanish from the assembly and reappear half-an-hour later chewing betel leaves. This whole makeshift and smoke-screen was an extremely distasteful procedure to every sensitive soul. If a man was heard to cry out, 'I would rather let my daughter remain unmarried than go through this,' the sentiment could well be understood seeing how important a place hospitality occupied in our scheme of life and how the celebration of a marriage was looked upon as an occasion when a man could make himself host to the entire town.

Fortunately all this is past. Now those who have daughters to marry may be heard to say, 'Fortunately there is no problem about rice now; only I must find the bridegroom. If I know how to get at him I could have the marriage done within twenty-four hours.'

*

Rice has brought back to our homes the lost hospitality. The doors of our 'guest-room' can be thrown open again without trepidation.

I met a foreigner who thought that the guest system in India worked on some such procedure as the following: a guest gave a month's advance notice saying, 'I shall be there between such and such a date; I shall be leaving again by such and such a train.' This supposition attacks the very basis of hospitality, its greatest charm being the element of surprise in it. In a household that practises the truest form of hospitality it is unnecessary to give any intimation of arrival. Giving a forewarning would be viewed as an unnecessary strain put upon a guest. A guest must have enough confidence that his sudden appearance on the threshold will not cause a nervous shock or a heart-attack, and that it will be taken with casual ease and even joy. The slightest consideration shown will look magnified in the eyes of a true guest. He may find no place other than the cement *pyol* abutting the street for sleeping in, but he will speak of it as if he had been provided with a four-poster and eiderdown, and a softly-curtained magic chamber for his repose at night. He may find that his hostess has served him only dilute buttermilk, and a most inedible piece of vegetable, but he will arise from his dining leaf with the air of one emerging from a banquet and call his host a man who takes a peculiar delight in watching the discomfiture of an overfed guest. The host for his part would say, 'I don't know if I have left you half-starving,' after actually serving a thirty-course dinner. Such a verbal exchange of courtesy between a guest and a host is a social necessity. The word *upacharam* means merely the verbal aspect of hospitality and the most important. A man may have neither milk nor sugar nor coffee powder at home but he must enquire, as soon as he has a visitor, 'May I give you coffee? Or would you prefer a little milk with sugar?' And the genuine guest will always reply, 'I just had everything. Even if you tempt me with a thousand sovereigns you cannot make me take a drop.'

*

The true host must know how much hospitality he should really exercise on a guest. So much depends upon the guests themselves. Some guests feel extremely uneasy if they are fussed about. They like to be left alone. A host must take a guest on his own terms. Some, especially those involved in a marriage celebration, like an excess of fuss. Even if the distinguished man is seen to be bursting with food it is the duty of the host to enquire: 'You don't look quite well. Are you on a diet? If I may provide you some special fare, please tell me.' A lapse in this regard is seldom forgiven, and many a marriage alliance has nearly been shattered on account of it. The true host walks on a razor's edge. An excess of a sense of hospitality is not a good thing either. A man I know is so eager to have guests that he nearly misbehaves when someone passes through the town without stopping at his house. It has embittered all his associations so much that in a few years' time, I fear, he will have no friends left. Hospitality is a sacred virtue, but has to be practised with circumspection, care, and in the right degree.

Everest Reactions

It was the youngest member of the household, Thumbi, now twelve years old, who came in with the news. He had gone out a little while earlier. It was his habit to go out and keep dashing in every little while with reports of Test scores, flying saucers, traffic accidents and other such matters. Today he came in crying, 'Everest has been conquered. They have reached the top.' People thought he was joking. Although generally an accurate reporter, occasionally, perhaps when he felt that people's interest in living was flagging, he tried to rouse them with stories of dacoity or arson in the neighbourhood, stories that would not bear a moment's scrutiny. Such tales would make the elders sit up and ask where he heard them and so forth, and the young man would go away pleased that he had succeeded in stirring his elders from their torpor. This seemed to be such an occasion. Thumbi tried to run away after declaring the conquest of Everest, but he was caught by the wrist and asked to explain.

'Where? Where? Who told you about it?'

'Got it over the radio in the next house.'

'Next house! How often have you been told to keep to your books and not loaf all over the place in the sun?'

'I was studying all afternoon and went out only for a moment to listen to the radio at the next house.'

'What has happened to our own radio?'

Finding that the subject was getting unnecessarily twisted, the young man declared, 'Everest has been climbed and that is all I know.'

'Don't be absurd!' cried his elders. 'Who has been telling you this cock-and-bull story?'

'I knew long ago that it would be climbed,' said Thumbi.

The elders groaned. 'How could it? How could could it be? It is impossible!'

'Tensing and Hillary have done it,' said the well-informed boy. He was delighted with his own success in impressing his elders. He added casually, 'They also find now that the height of Everest had all along been mistaken. It is about a thousand feet more than what it was thought to be.'

'Impossible! Who has been putting ideas into your head?' cried the elders.

'How do you know all this, boy? It was only yesterday that we heard that the assault was to be given up.'

'But there it is,' said the precocious boy triumphantly. 'Hillary and Tensing . . .' The elders took in the news with a sort of gloomy resignation. This was a piece of news for which the world had waited for a century or more and now, instead of arriving in a spectacular manner with a fanfare of trumpets, it was reaching them through Thumbi—that habitual purveyor of news titbits.

Soon they had to accept it for a fact. For the rest of the day, they were bandying about expressions such as cwm and col, no two persons agreeing on the definition of these expressions or their origin.

Their reactions were interesting to watch. Somehow there was a general sense of disappointment at the fact that Everest had been conquered. It would have been so nice to have left Everest as an unassailable part of the earth. Said one, 'It is not good to think that human beings have conquered everything under the sun. It does a lot of good to the human spirit to feel that there are still many things beyond our reach. Human beings should not become so proud.'

Said an enthusiast, 'A masterpiece of planning. It restores one's faith in human endeavour. Clear-headed planning is the most difficult thing to achieve. I challenge anyone here to plan a journey to Tirupati and get through it without having to alter it half-a-dozen times on the way.'

'It depends,' said another, 'on inaugurating the whole thing at the right moment from an astrologer's point of view. The secret of success lies in getting the horoscope of the persons concerned and fixing the time accordingly. If it is done accurately it will solve ninety per cent of the difficulties of any undertaking.'

'And so no marks for preparation, knowledge, study, and scientific application and so forth?'

'Even a study becomes successful only when it is begun at the right moment. I am sure they must have avoided *rahukalam* and other inauspicious moments while beginning their arrangements. I am going to write to Col. Hunt to send the horoscopes of the members of the expedition and also to tell me the exact hour at which they started their preparations. Astrology is a great science, sir.'

'Now that they have made a start,' began another, 'I believe going to Everest will become common. It may almost become a holiday resort. It is going to be difficult to come across a person who has not had a holiday on Everest.'

'With so much ice,' said another with a business temperament, 'suppose they find some means of quarrying all that ice and sending it down! It will revolutionize the cold-storage industry completely. Ultimately it may become necessary to rehabilitate the members now attached to refrigeration and air-conditioning industries.'

'Whatever geographers might say,' said another, 'we cannot help feeling that Everest is in India. Even Tensing, do you know, is an Indian?'

'I won't be happy until I hear that an Indian expedition has planted its flag on Everest,' said another.

'How are you sure that someone is not already at it. By logical methods we can do many things: we could climb the highest peak without any special equipment. There are more things in heaven and . . .'

'Oh, stop, stop. I won't hear that quotation again. I am tired of it.'

Further discussion on this subject was stopped when Thumbi burst in in his usual lightning manner with the announcement, 'My friend's father who had gone out hunting last night, it seems, has bagged five tigers simultaneously. . .'

Cruelty to Children[*]

In the stress of the concerns of the adult world, the problems or rather the plight of children pass unnoticed. I am not referring to any particular class but to childhood itself. The hardship starts right at home, when straight from sleep the child is pulled out and got ready for school even before its faculties are awake. He (or she) is groomed and stuffed into a uniform and packed off to school with a loaded bag on his back. The school-bag has become an inevitable burden for the child. I am now pleading for abolition of the school-bag, as a national policy, by an ordinance if necessary. I have investigated and found that an average child carries strapped to his back, like a pack-mule, not less than six to eight kgs of books, notebooks and other paraphernalia of modern education in addition to lunch-box and water bottle. Most children on account of this daily burden develop a stoop and hang their arms forward like a chimpanzee while walking, and I know cases of serious spinal injuries in some children too. Asked why not leave some books behind at home, the child explains it is her teacher's orders that all books and notes must be brought every day to the class, for what reason God alone knows. If there is a lapse, the child invites punishment, which takes the form of being rapped on the knuckles with a wooden scale, a refinement from our days when we received cane cuts on the palm only. The child is in such terror of the teacher, whether known as Sister, Mother Superior, or just Madam, that he or she is prepared to carry out any command issued by the teacher, who has no imagination or sympathy.

The dress regulation particularly in convent schools is another senseless formality—tie and laced shoes and socks, irrespective of the climate, is compulsory. Polishing a shoe and lacing it becomes a major task for a child first thing in the day. When the tie has become an anachronism even in the adult world, it's absurd to enforce it on children. A simple uniform and footwear must be designed and brought into force and these should be easier to maintain.

[*] Narayan's maiden speech as a Member of Parliament delivered at the Rajya Sabha in 1989.

After school hours when the child returns home her mother or home tutor is waiting to pounce on her, snatch her bag and compel her to go through some special coaching or homework. For the child the day has ended; with no time left for her to play or dream. It is a cruel, harsh life imposed on her, and I present her case before this house for the honourable members to think out and devise remedies by changing the whole educational system and outlook so that childhood has a chance to bloom rather than wilt in the process of learning.

Other areas where the child needs protection is from involvement in adult activities such as protest marches, parades, or lining up on road-sides for waving in VIPs; children are made to stand in the hot sun for hours without anyone noticing how much they suffer from fatigue, hunger and thirst. Children must be protected, and cherished which would seem especially relevant in this year of the Nehru centenary. How it is to be done is upto our rulers and administrators to consider—perhaps not by appointing a commission of enquiry, but in some other practical and peaceful manner.

The Postcard

In a fickle and fluctuating world, the postcard alone has retained its identity, though a victim of a sort of caste system operating in the world of letter writing. I have heard people say, 'I never write on a postcard nor accept one, but tell the postman to take it back. . . .' I am sorry to say that such snobs will not hesitate to use a whole sheet of crackling note-paper for a couple of lines of acknowledgement, and ceremoniously tuck it into a parchment envelope.

I must confess that I too was guilty of ignoring the postcard for years out of a cowardly feeling that it might offend the receiver. But suddenly I had a flash of illumination the other day, of all places, at the Bangalore airport, having driven a hundred miles to catch a plane for Delhi at noon which didn't show up even at five p.m.

At the counter, the officials sounded grumpy and scowled as if the passengers had cast some sort of a spell and immobilized their Air Bus. The public address system was not of much help either—it kept up a series of throaty growls which did not add much to our information; a black board at the Enquiry evidently bore a message for us but chalky writing on rubbed-off chalky writing demanded a kind of scrutiny for which my eyesight was not equal, especially when a hundred others were also going through the same drill. And so I was forced to slip into a state of semi-coma and resignation.

Nowhere on earth could weariness overwhelm one as at an airport 'wait'. For a while you enjoy the spectacle of fellow passengers, burdened with baggage and restless children, looking for seats or in various attitudes of abandonment in the lounge. Presently one tires of looking at the same set of faces round after round, tires of the bookstall and the restaurant, gets bored with the funny comments on air travel everyone is uttering and concludes that this is perhaps a foretaste of purgatory while the gods take their time to decide whether to send one to hell or heaven.

It was in this state of mind that I peeped through the little window at the postoffice counter. The man on the other side asked, 'What do you want?'

On an impulse I said, 'Postcards, please.'

'How many?'

'Ten.'

And there it was. I sought a secluded corner and settled down to write, and addressed and dropped the cards into the mail-box, thus clearing arrears of correspondence weighing on my conscience for months. I bought more cards and dashed off greetings, congratulations and condolences, on a mass scale, in flight. Since that day, I have set myself up as a promoter of the postcard.

Among its advantages: You don't have to be longwinded on a card: you could write a one line note to your correspondent and be done with it. No one will mind it. On the other hand if you choose to be expansive, you can write two hundred words on the back of the postcard and one hundred on the space in front, through measured, careful calligraphy. In olden times our noble ancestors wrote only on postcards. They filled a card without wasting a hair-breadth's space. Starting from a millimetre margin on top with 'Safe' or '*Om*' etched minutely, they progressed, line by line, and then also in the half-space on the address-side right down to the bottom edge of the card—thereafter the card was held breadthwise and all second thoughts were crammed along a slender margin, as also blessings and the signature.

Marriages were no doubt made in heaven, but were translated into earthly terms only through postcards. Marriage proposals were initiated and conducted through an exchange of postcards: the 'bio-data' of the principals, their background and lineage, extending to four generations, the disposition of the stars, as well as complicated negotiations relating to dowry, silver, gold, brass, stainless steel, and silks, and specifications of the dimensions and quantity of *murukku*, and details of wedding and travel arrangements were all satisfactorily concluded on this humble stationery. Nothing ever went wrong, and thousands of couples lived happily ever after.

The chief merit of a card is that it circulates in an open society. No secrets are possible. Everyone could know everything about everyone else in a family and anyone's business became a matter of general discussion, comment and advice. Even the postman used to be aware of the contents of a card before delivering it. If some auspicious event was taking place at a particular address, such as a birthday or a betrothal, the postman would delay the delivery of any unpleasant news. In my boyhood at Puraswalkam (Madras) over half-a-century ago, we had a postman, an old man in a red turban and khaki uniform, called Thanappa. When schools closed for summer, on any day we could anticipate his announcement from the door, holding out a card, 'Periamma, your daughter in Bangalore is coming with the children on the 10th of this month, so get ready.' Or to a young student who had his lodging in our house, 'You have failed again! No wonder. I see you always at the street corner gossiping. Why don't you study properly, instead of wasting your time, with your father worrying so much about you in the village.'

Correspondence has been a matter of despair for me and equally so for my correspondents. I generally put off answering letters while I wait for the arrival of the typist and other propitious conditions. Dictation, scrutiny of the draft, and all the labour of sealing, glueing and stamping, terrifies me, and I put off answering letters as far as possible. Now it is all changed. With a postcard, all intermediary activities are abolished. You just dash off a line or two, turn it over, write the address, and drop it in any wayside postbox. It is pilfer-proof. Nobody has any use for a used postcard.

Lastly, by confining oneself to postcards and avoiding the more expensive postal stationery, one may defeat the aim of the budget-framers, who seem bent upon mopping up your cash. The 'hike', (what a popular but hybrid expression, of petro-dollar parentage) in postal rates may be nullified by writing only a postcard for every occasion. You may carry on thus safely, until the government wakes up and levies a 'surcharge', (or would it be a 'cess'?) on every word beyond a free allowance of twenty. If that happens, further action would still remain in your hands. Don't write letters. Avoid all correspondence.

As I am closing, a card arrives, on which I see a red seal indicating that this is the centenary year of the postcard (1979). It is sheer coincidence. I'd had no idea of it when I began this essay. May the postcard continue to serve us for centuries to come.

The Cat

Among animals, I admire the cat for its poise and equanimity. Except when some important issue is to be argued out with an intruder from another territory, and that mostly at midnight seated on a wall, at all other times it is very silent and composed, soft in movement and unobtrusive, taking good care to avoid being noticed. Among human beings it may have a favourite whom it will greet by arching the back and mewing in an undertone, sometimes going to the lengths of brushing against his leg too. That is all. Never more demonstrative than that.

Recently at the Madras Music Academy, during the festival, I sat with a thousand others and tried to listen to the music, but it was not always easy, since there is a habit among our people of moving about and carrying on conversation during a concert, not exactly in whispers but a little above the *sruti* of the singer struggling to establish his voice in that vast hall.

In contrast to the human behaviour, a cat sat on the platform, perfectly still, facing the singer. I noticed him only on the evening of D.K. Jayaraman's performance, but learnt later that he would be present on the platform every evening, especially at the prime hour between 5 and 7.30. He sat so still that one could mistake him for a decorative piece. Sometimes he sat with his head half-turned towards the auditorium, quietly watching the public in their seats, but looking at no one in particular, very much in the style of a VIP chairman. At some point he would tuck in his limbs and tail and shut his eyes in total relaxation, displaying a model behaviour in a music hall.

He was not generally noticed because of his unobtrusive manners as well as his perfect camouflage: he merged perfectly in his surrounding of sombre carpets and saree patterns of the assembly on the platform. Nature had endowed him with a coat of grey and black, with a dash of yellow, and polka dots here and there, rather difficult to specify his complexion in a single phrase. He merged into his background while he was there, but suddenly at some point he would not be there, so smoothly making his exit that you might wonder if you had suffered a hallucination all along. During subsequent studies, I discovered the exact point at which he would vanish. During *thani avarthanam* of mridangam, especially if the percussion maestro belonged to the hard-hitting class and generated enormous decibels out of his instrument. At such times the cat hastily picked himself up and raced down the wooden steps of the platform. (He never committed the indignity of jumping away while in the hall, but, though in a hurry to leave, carried himself with poise proper to the occasion.) He avoided the place during Bharatha Natyam performances, feeling perhaps that so much of stamping of feet and convulsive movements are not conducive to a peaceful evening for a cat. He avoided the morning sessions too when there would be much excited talk and debate. At such times, I have noticed him curled up under a chair in the Special Reserved Class, away from the platform.

Others who have noticed the cat speculate that he might be a savant or maestro of the last century preferring this guise so that he might arrive and depart without fuss or embarrassment to the management. (Incidentally you may remember how God Indra assumed the form of a cat, in order to try and slip away when the husband of the woman in his arms arrived home suddenly.) There is also a view that the Academy cat might be an ancient musician who never made it to Sangeeta Kalanidhi though he aspired and manoeuvred for it all his life.

But for me such notions are far-fetched. I see no harm in taking a cat for a cat. Why not? As good a creation of God as anything else. Man in his arrogance concludes it is impossible for a cat to enjoy music. He cannot tolerate the idea of music appealing to a cat unless he anthropomorphises the creature. To me this is just a cat with an ear for music and respect for the institution. However when he folds up, shuts his eyes and remains immobile, even during a dull patch in the concert, he may not express disapproval, out of good manners, but might just switch off his mind and turn his thoughts to the mice scuttling under the wooden platform or he may brood over his affairs in the alley: For, though he is seen in the Academy, it is not his home. I have noticed him at midnight going up the corridor of the deluxe block of the Woodlands Hotel nearby, and I learnt from the watchman that this cat belongs to the hotel but enjoys a wide jurisdiction. I think he creates the same illusion in the hotel next door, in the next two bungalows, as well as at the Music Academy, of belonging to each place. T.S. Eliot, who shows profound understanding of cats, mentions in his *Book of Cats* a particular cat who was a conjuror and could create an illusion of being at several places at the same time.

Red-taping Culture

'Culture' is a vague expression, employed widely and understood in different ways, but it is handy and sounds respectable. Like the quality of mercy it's twice blessed—blesseth him that gives and him that takes. No one would, normally, demand a definition of the term. In my college days, I remember a professor of cultural history saying on the very first day, 'What is culture? We know agriculture, sericulture and apiculture or any blessed culture with a prefix. But just 'culture' is an elusive term. We teachers have to manage somehow, according to our own inclination and equipment; a seasoned archaeologist can create culture with pieces of pottery, coins and beads dug out from under layers of ancient dust. We historians have to base our conclusions on the labours of sycophants at the courts who chronicled for their survival the glorious deeds of ancient despots. Social anthropologists have developed their own jargon based on field studies, kinship charts, and so forth. It is all a laborious and indefinite pursuit and one has to sympathize with culture-dealers who try to give a shape to an abstract something.'

Where academic professors have to labour hard for mining culture, the bureaucrat takes it in his stride (especially after 'culture' has become State property), and he can deliver neat, categorized packages of culture tied in red-tape. Presently, there may come up an imposing edifice named Culture Bhavan in Delhi. One may look forward to hearing the following conversation at the enquiry counter.

'Yes?'

'I want culture.'

'Instant or regular?'

'What's instant?'

'For personal and family purposes. Regular is for export. Fill up the yellow form if you want folk. . .'

'What's folk? Aren't we all folks? Who is in the special category of folk?'

'No time for any discussion. You will find all the relevant information in the folder—study it carefully and come tomorrow—if you are interested in bronzes, fill the red form—you'll have to produce I.T.C. Certificate and export permits. . .'

'What's I.T.C?'

'Read the folder—all forms should be completed in triplicate. Write your father's name in full and your mother's maiden name. . .'

'But they are no more. . .'

'In that case, file their death certificates with your application. After it is processed, we will work out an estimate—and subsidize a part of it in pursuance of our policy to encourage private effort.'

'If our countryside dances and entertainments are performed out of their context and background, will they not look grotesque and unconvincing, against, say, the Eiffel Tower? Secondly, how can bronze images be uprooted from the shrines where they are installed with so much ceremony? Will it be proper?'

'Are your doubts genuine?'

'Yes, sir.'

'Then you should go to the Doubts Clearance Cell on the third floor and present your doubts in writing. . .'

'More forms to be filled?'

'No, no. You may write on blank paper on one side—only a notarized attestation will be needed for your signature. . .'

'One more question please! What will it cost me?'

'A crore or two—more or less. Don't bother about it at this stage. However, if you have financial questions, go to the fourth floor, but remember, the lift is out of order.'

*

Following last year's Humour Conference in Hyderabad, I suffer from a growing anxiety that some day humour may become nationalized and packaged. A Central Circular may emanate on the following lines:

Confidential: To all District Heads:

It has been found desirable to compile a roster of humorous men in our country. You are requested to submit a list of jokers, clowns, buffoons, raconteurs, and wits in your area.

All officials should immediately realize:

(a) That they are part of a humorous community and conduct themselves accordingly, the policy being that laughter, rather than grimness or gloom, makes for efficiency in public service.

(b) Humour is the natural entitlement of every citizen, rich or poor, and must begin at the grass-roots and spread into a broad spectrum.

(c) Elitism and subtlety must be minimized, if not discouraged. Humour must be aimed at the weaker sections and similar categories who may be in need of immediate relief.

(d) Spontaneous laughter may be generally authorized but care must be taken not to be misled by every grin and simper.

(e) Minimal infrastructure with staff in appropriate uniforms (for grading and inspection of the quantum of available humour) must be built up without delay. Budgetary proposals for this purpose must be submitted for allocation of grants under the general heading 'culture'.

Family Doctor

I fear the grand old institution of 'family doctor' is now gone. I say 'doctor', rather than 'physician' or 'surgeon', since no one ever bothered about such distinctions in the good old times. 'Doctor' was a generic term without a category or classification, and also the family doctor of pre-War years lived up to our expectations of his being an all-round healer.

That was before medical science developed complex branches. There was little popular writing on health, disease and sudden mortality: too much information has now created hypochondriacs who suspect the worst at the least symptom of pain and rush to the doctor for an opinion, who cannot help suggesting, 'Why don't you go through a complete check-up and see me again?' The man appears again before his doctor in due course, clutching a sheaf of documents and papers, like a habitual litigant at a lawyer's office, to be assured by the doctor in most cases, 'You are fine. Nothing to worry about.'

The present-day doctor has to make sure that he has scientific backing before pronouncing an opinion. But the old family doctor gave the same cheerful verdict spontaneously, intuitively, without much ado. Probing and scanning being unheard of, he had to depend for diagnosis on a stethoscope, thermometer and a flashlight, and probably a spoon to hold down the tongue for examining a throat. Also, by tapping the abdomen and chest with two fingers, he could judge from the subtle resonance what might be right and wrong under the skin. His final advice would be, 'Avoid buttermilk and drink plenty of water,' or he might sit down and write a prescription, perhaps in Latin, with an air of one composing a sonnet, to be interpreted only by the pharmacist later, who would fill an eight-ounce bottle with a colourful mixture labelled properly. A bazaar doctor of my acquaintance, whose clients were mostly villagers, wrote his prescriptions in not less than twenty minute lines and then turned the sheet sideways and wrote also on the margin while his patients looked on solemnly, in profound admiration.

Tablets and antibiotics in aluminium strips were unknown in those days. In case of pneumonia, I remember fermentation with what seemed to be warmed-up horse manure (judging from the pervasive odour) was recommended. For eye trouble, which is nowadays handled by specialists with extreme delicacy, our doctor would just turn up the patient's eye-lids and rub on silver nitrate every morning while the patient groaned and squirmed. Occasionally, in an emergency, the doctor would also hold down the patient and incise an abscess with a scalpel and soak the wound in tincture iodine while the patient screamed and cursed and tried to knock down the doctor. However, relief was definite in most cases, achieved through an unflinching faith in the family doctor and the doctor's faith that we would not so easily crumble or collapse, which speaks for the hardihood of the human constitution.

There was an indefinable quality and sustenance in the relationship between a doctor and his patient, which is missing today. Nowadays every doctor is hard-pressed for time with an unrelenting 'Kumbh Mela' crowd at his door night and day. The doctor-patient relationship has become literally mechanical. At a busy doctor's establishment, you will come face to face with the doctor, if at all, only at the end of a long journey through a number of secretaries, technicians and assistants.

I have come to this conclusion after a recent experience with an ear specialist after a great deal of importuning over the phone. At the waiting hall, by the time my name was called, I had finished reading cover to cover several old issues of a ladies' journal heaped on the table. I presented myself at a ticket window. On the other side a lady was sitting and questioned me as to what was wrong and took down dictation while I narrated my troubles through the grill. Next, I was ushered into the presence of the doctor who studied my card, examined my ear and gestured to me to follow his assistant. I found myself in a chamber of electronics. The operators seated me on a stool and turned switches off and on after fitting an ear-phone to me, and finally produced a chart on graph paper. Back to the doctor, who studied the chart, handed me a printed message which just confirmed that I was having an ear problem, but assured that it was inevitable at my age, and concluded with the advice that I take B-Complex daily. I wanted clarification on some points in the printed message but I realized that the next patient was already breathing down my neck. And 'I came out by the same door as in I went', my head throbbing with unasked questions.

Causerie

My little niece, Shanta, went on repeating the ditty:

> *Nicely want, nicely want;*
> *Shame, shame; poppy shame;*
> *All the girls know your name.*

I noticed her uttering these lines whenever she found us lost in some little predicament such as having a pencil point broken while signing, or losing in a game, or getting snubbed unexpectedly. I tried to analyze its meaning. Evidently it was her way (as well as that of her companions) of gloating over another's moment of awkward plight.

From this general understanding, I tried to make out a particular meaning. What was 'nicely want?' A phrase which looked so agreeable could not possibly have any unpleasant meaning. But after much questioning I found out that it was a literal translation of a vernacular idiom *nanna venum* said by one who watched, unsympathetically of course, someone else in trouble; example, a younger brother watching the ears of his bullying elder brother being twisted by the arithmetic teacher; the idiom indicates a state of mild vindictiveness and the satisfaction arising therefrom. No one who has no sense of our own idiom could ever understand the statement. It is one hundred per cent *swadeshi* like the towers of our temple or our *rasam*.

What was 'poppy shame'? I asked, for enlightenment, and the little girl at first said that she did not know, but later explained that it was 'like the poppy flower'. How many of us have seen poppy flowers? Is it poppy of the drug or of the flower garden? Does it signify oblivion to everything except the state of shame such as '... of hemlock drunk and half a minute ago had letheward sunk?' Or if it is the harmless flower-bed poppy, it perhaps means a little embarrassment, delicate and finely-patterned like the poppy flower; just enough to make one blush to the tint of a poppy in the garden and no more? What really intrigued me was 'All the girls know your name'. I thought no boy would mind that, whatever may be the reaction of girls to the prospect; but the little girl disillusioned my mind by spelling it out. She said it was 'no' your name not 'know'. Ah, could it mean that word was used as a verb without an auxiliary? 'All the girls "no" your name' might be a picturesque way of saying that all the girls will cry 'no' in one voice the moment your name is mentioned. Does it mean they won't accept any date in the modern sense or is it a relic of the old *swayamwara* days when a girl could say yes or no unmistakably? I am still thinking of this verse. Anyway it holds a pretty dreadful prospect for one fallen from grace.

*

I read of a country in which there were so many holidays that the dates of the calendar were generally printed in red, the working dates being indicated by a small sprinkling of black letters. I think we are fast approaching this stage. On one side, there is talk of the Five Year Plan and its urgency; on the other side our readiness to pull down the shutter any minute. Religious occasions, the birth or death of eminent men (in some instances the date of someone's birth is celebrated without prejudice to the observance of his date of death later), Saints' Days, National Celebrations (two sets again), and several New Year Days. I do not wish to be a killjoy but I do want to be able to receive my mail in time and to ask for my cash at the bank for the maximum number of days possible in a year. A very urgent communication which I had been expecting arrived on the 14th of August, but I was not at home when the registered packet arrived; the 15th of August was a holiday, on the 16th the postman could not get at me again; he had left the postoffice when I went there in search of him; he had left our area when I went back to look for him. In this hide-and-seek another day was lost, the 17th was a holiday again; on the 18th our usual postman had a headache and a substitute was sent who delayed so long in finding each address that the letter missed me again. There was no use in my going to postoffice because it was a Saturday and the shutters were down at one p.m. The 19th was a Sunday. I succeeded in taking charge of my urgent letter on the 20th (after a delay of nearly a week) by presenting myself at the postoffice at 6 a.m. long before anyone should leave the building. I leave the subject there without further comment.

*

A recent essay I wrote on the cosmic nature of the white ant's activity has brought me much support. I have been receiving lists of articles consumed by the white ant. Going over the lists I am more than ever convinced that there is a design and plan in the activities of the white ant. A friend who was addicted to playing on the 'leg harmonium' went away on a holiday after pushing his instrument into a corner and covering it with a blanket. After his holiday when he wanted to resume his musical exercise, he found the white keys left suspended in mid-air as from a ghost musical-box; the bellows as well as the box portion of the harmonium were gone. This no doubt distressed the harmonium player himself but brought immeasurable relief and joy to his neighbours.

A devoted husband cherished the heavy crayon drawings and the garish watercolours done by his wife, and compelled his friends to appreciate them whenever they made the mistake of visiting him. The wife was a prolific artist, the husband's devotion knew no limit, the friends suffered acutely and began to drop off. It threatened to create tension between the gentleman and his good friends. Luckily for the friend, white ants got into the almirah in which the art treasures were kept. Presently, it was discovered that all the crayon work as well as watercolours had been impartially devoured. The lady lost heart and took a vow never to touch a paint-box again. The friends resumed their visits.

*

The brightest piece of news for the week has been the placing of the English language on 'Open General Licence' again. Till now we had worked ourselves into a position where the language took on the aspect of a contraband article. To change the metaphor, the English language was almost like an outlaw who could not be actually outlawed. We saw him here, we saw him there, we saw him everywhere, but no one could do anything about it. You fulminated against him, you denounced him unreservedly, and you put a price on his head but still he moved about unconcerned with an air that things would be all right in the end. In our dislike of Imperialism we made the mistake of identifying the language with the Imperialist. One might as well forswear all military uniform because our English rulers wore them. But the language itself has an independent colonizing habit: it goes 'native', and becomes so rooted in the soil that it cannot be uprooted. Let us thank providence that this fact has now been recognized and that we may speak and write this language without feeling all the time that we are engaged in an un-national activity.

MALGUDI SKETCHES AND STORIES

Over a Mountain Range

From Arisikere the approach to Kadur is not very inspiring. Through the train window one sees mostly monotonous undulating fields, clusters of cactus, blunt rocks, odd boulders piled up anyhow, and fields covered with ashen, stunted scrub. It is rather disappointing because I have heard so much about the beauty of this district. The sandy, rocky undulations with their ruffian vegetation seem to me a very discouraging sample. But craning out of the window and looking towards the engine, I see far away blue outlines shimmering in the heat haze, but my sense of survey being poor it doesn't seem very convincing to me that I should be there in a few hours.

Outside the station at Kadur I take my seat in a bus, in gloomy resignation. It is a discoloured, rattling vehicle with the look of a camel about to take on the last straw; hot passengers are pressed and packed in every seat; the oblique rays of the sun enter the bus and scorch our faces and hands; outside, the eye can rest only on clusters of uninteresting shops, a meaningless patch of ground with burnt grass on it, and a dilapidated bus office; the bus is always about to start but never really starts, only the bus conductor's shouting gathers volume and speed; it is not a moment very conducive to a cheerful outlook on life. I am one of the two privileged to sit beside the driver, the main recompense there being (if you don't mind your feet shrivelling up in the engine heat) that you needn't twist and fold up your legs but can stretch them, and look, not at the suffering faces of fellow-passengers, but at the land in front of you.

The bus has not journeyed half-an-hour when I notice a change in the surroundings; in front stretches away a green, shaded avenue with lawns on the sides; we are gradually passing into jungle country. The road goes up and curves; the bus is climbing a gradient; the air cools, and the surroundings soften. Mound after mound of green thicket, bamboo clusters as far as the eye can see. What a haven for a big game lover! I casually drop an enquiry, vaguely recollecting a notice 'Caught in Kadur Forests' over a tiger cage in the Mysore Zoo. 'Plenty of them,' my neighbour assures me. 'You can see them on the roadside if you come by the night bus.

They are majestic things, they just get up and stand aside to let the bus pass.' I am content to take his word for it.

A bus-stop. Most of the passengers jump down, throw their limbs about, and drink coconuts at a wayside shop. I see a finger-post on the branch road with the inscription 'Sakkrepatna' on it; and it stirs up associations in the mind. Wasn't this the capital of King Rukmangadha? We slide back a few thousand years: now comes to mind the story of the waterman who stopped a flood with his life. Four miles west of Sakkrepatna is Ayyankere, a magnificent reservoir formed by embanking a perennial stream at the foot of Sakunagiri. It is a deep tank with thirty-five feet of water in some places, and the embankment is 1,700 feet long and 300 feet high. Once the tank was about to breach, and it was revealed to the waterman in a dream by the guardian Goddess of the tank. He pleaded with the Goddess and made her promise that she would not breach it till he ran up to Sakkrepatna, informed the king, and returned with his orders. The king on hearing of it realized that the only way to prevent the catastrophe would be to prevent the return of the waterman forever, and so had him killed on the spot. The tank was saved; it is still intact, and there is a shrine at Sakkrepatna erected to the memory of this waterman.

The sudden sounding of the bus horn jerks one back to the present. The bus driver becomes impatient with the coconut drinkers and threatens that unless they come running back to their seats before the next sounding of the horn, he will leave them to their coconuts and go forward.

At four o'clock in the evening we reach Chickmagalur. According to certain traditions this was a dowry bestowed on his younger daughter by King Rukmangadha, and he gave his elder daughter Hiremagalur, which is a mile off. Hiremagalur is identified as the place where Janamejaya of the *Mahabharata* performed a great serpent sacrifice in order to avenge the death of his father from snake-bite. There is a stone pillar at the spot where the sacrifice was performed, and the belief is that a person bitten by a snake can ward off the poison if he goes round this pillar after a bath in a nearby pond.

Chickmagalur nestles in a valley south of Bababuden Range, and looking about from here one is struck by the number of hill ranges that stretch away in wave after wave on all sides. The town itself is very attractive with its bright, new buildings, vast open grounds, its tree-covered slopes, and parks. You feel here that if you go beyond the town limits you may step off into blue, empty space. This town is really a jumping off ground for an excursion through the most impressive mountain country in Mysore state.

Next I am in a bus which is to take me to Kemmangandi, one of the highest points in the Bababuden Range. The road passes through dense coffee estates, wriggles at the foot of towering mountain slopes, and over the edge of valleys covered with immense stretches of forests. At every turn, in the distance fantastic mountain peaks rear up, keep us company for a mile or two and recede; the most prominent of them being *Kudre-Mukh* or Horse-face, so named on account of its appearance. It is the loftiest peak in this part of the Western Ghats and from time immemorial a familiar landmark to navigators on the West Coast.

On this road, about eight miles from Chickmagalur, there is the tomb of an ancient Mohammedan saint from whom this range takes its name. To do him justice we must think of him whenever we drink coffee. It was he who first introduced coffee into India. When he took up his residence at this place he brought with him a few seeds from Mocha and planted them for his use. Every coffee plant that stands on any hill slope in India today is a great-great-grandchild of the first plant that Bababuden reared. The cave containing his tomb is very sacred to Mohammedans. This cave is equally sacred to Hindus, who believe that Dattatreya disappeared into it ages ago and will reappear on the day Vishnu incarnates as Kalki before the Deluge.

In the evening the bus precipitates me at Kemmangandi and disappears in a cloud of red dust. This is a tiny hill station at a height of 4,752 feet above sea level. It captures a traveller's heart at first sight—its neat red roads winding up, hedged by lovely plants; its garden and woodland schemes; the quiet beauty of the building belonging to the Palace; and the footpaths mysteriously going up and down, leading to the valleys and grassy uplands and forests. Here live half-a-dozen officials belonging to the Palace, Bhadravathi Iron Works, and to the Forest Department. These are a set of robust cheerful souls perfectly happy in their mountain home, not in the least worried about the outside world, and completely absorbed in their work: the forest officer suddenly appears from some jungle and vanishes before daybreak into it once again; the Palace officials tend the garden and the buildings; the Bhadravathi people blast the mountainside and load the ore in buckets which roll down a cableway into the valley below.

The great event in their daily life is the arrival of a bus morning and evening. Their attuned ears catch the bus sound a mile off, and they are on the road when it arrives, eagerly looking for their newspapers, mail bag, and for a possible visitor.

These people are fanatically devoted to the place and won't allow a single word of doubt to cross one's lips: 'Mosquitoes? Mosquitoes are unheard of things here. You will never catch a cold here. Drink our water and it will cure you of all ills.' I casually mention that I am proceeding next to Gersoppa Falls. The young man who is my host looks almost shocked and denounces even the mighty Gersoppa Falls. They are all agreed that Gersoppa is a sadly over-rated business: 'You must see the falls we have up here, falling down three hundred feet.'

'How far is it?'

'About three miles. The climb is worth it; if you see it you will never go near Gersoppa Falls again.' I wish I had the energy and the time to go up and see this rival to Gersoppa. And then my friend tells me about some strange herbal plot, about half-a-furlong in length, a walk through which is a cure for a heavy stomach. You may eat the richest stuff, but a walk through the path will digest it, and you will have to go back and eat again, you may come again and digest it, and go back and fill your stomach once more .... There is a magic property in this atmosphere,' declares the young man fervently.

I spend a part of the night gazing at the dark valley in front of the veranda, and far away beyond a ridge the skyline is lit up as if by a full moon below; these are the lights of Shimoga town about thirty miles away.

The next morning I notice great activity in a neighbouring house, much calling, shouting, and excitement. 'What is the matter?' I ask. 'The barber is come,' announces my friend. He tells me that a wandering barber comes from Shimoga or somewhere occasionally, and when he is seen he is held up, and everyone has his hair cut and calls up his friends. There is no knowing when the barber will come next so that while the opportunity lasts everyone has his hair cut, and cut as short as possible.

They reluctantly allow me to go when the bus arrives, only on my promise that I will visit them again (which I hope I shall be able to fulfil some day).

'What other things can I see here?' I ask.

'We won't tell you. You can spend a whole week here. You had better come again and see for yourself. Your book won't be complete unless you devote a whole section of it to Kemmangandi.'

'All right,' I promise lightly and get into the bus, and they stand on the road waving till the bus is out of sight.

Sringeri

About twelve centuries ago Sankara was born at Kaladi (near Cochin) of parents who had been childless for long. They had been praying night and day for an issue. In answer to their prayer Shiva appeared in the guise of an old man, in a dream, and asked, 'Do you want numerous children who live a hundred years but who are dullards and evil-doers or only one son who is exceptionally gifted but who will live with you for only a short time?' The mother rejected mere quantity. Sankara was born, with only sixteen years as his allotted span of life. In his fifth year he learnt the *Gayatri* and underwent spiritual and other disciplines; in his eighth year he mastered all the *Shastras*, *Puranas*, *Vedas*, *Vedanta*, and *Sutras*. And a little later he renounced the world and donned the ochre robe.

The rest of his life is the record of a great teacher. Through his writings, debates and talks, he spread far and wide his *advaita* philosophy—a doctrine which says that all that exists is a particle of a great soul and merges in the end in that soul. 'His was the task of ending the nightmare of separateness,' says one of his commentators.

After travelling extensively he came to Sringeri. Sringeri had already been sanctified by the presence of great sages like Vasishta, Viswamitra, Vibhandaka, Kasyapa, and others, who had their *ashrams* in its forests and performed *tapas*. A look at this place will make us understand why it was so favoured, a place surrounded with green hilltops and immense forests, and watered by the river Tunga, which is considered to be more sacred than any other river in the world. If Ganga springs from Vishnu's feet, Tunga springs from his face, and the gods are said to bathe in it.

Before making up his mind to settle here Sankaracharya stood on the right bank of the river and looked about. This spot is now marked by a little shrine. He had in his hand the golden image of Sharada or Saraswathi, the Goddess of Knowledge and Culture, for whom he was going to build a temple, which was to be the central power-house, so to speak, of his philosophy and the institution which was born of it. At his feet Tunga flowed, its water turned silvery by the rays of the midday sun. As he stood observing the surroundings Sankaracharya beheld a sight on the opposite bank which thrilled him and made him realize that he had come to the end of his journey. A cobra spread its hood and held it like an umbrella over a frog, protecting it from the heat of the sun. 'This is the place!' Sankaracharya said on seeing it. 'Here is harmony, an absence of hatred even among creatures which are natural enemies.' Even today on the river-step a tiny niche made of a couple of stones marks the spot where this phenomenon was seen. The niche is filled with mud and sand but a slight excavation with fingers will reveal the cobra and the frog carved on a stone.

Sankaracharya crossed the river. This village was henceforth to be of vital importance to humanity, its significance to last beyond the reckoning of time. Hence he first proceeded to build four guardian temples in the surrounding hillocks, which were to protect the place from all possible dangers, diseases and evils. On the eastern hillock he built a temple for Kalabhairava, on the western hillock for Anjaneya, on the southern hillock for Durgi, and on the northern for Kali. Even today worship is being performed thrice a day in these temples. The people of Sringeri have strong faith in the protection that these guardians afford. I had a surprising instance of it from the person who was acting as my guide and who was a vaccinator. During our walk he casually mentioned that there were a few cases of typhoid in the town. When I asked him what measures they were taking to combat it he said, 'We are quite confident that none of these cases will turn fatal. My daughter too had an attack of it and a relapse, and its only effect has been the loss of hair. As long as we have these,' he pointed at the temples on the hillocks, 'we have nothing to fear. In summer we have a few cases of small-pox too. But there is nothing to worry or fear. This place is protected. If any of the cases turns fatal it will be due to extraordinary *karma,* and nothing can be done about it.' I admired his grand faith; all the same I could not help pressing upon him the need for giving widespread anti-typhoid injections. He at once made a note of it. Though this incident is trivial it indicated to me a certain resilience and breadth of mind and an absence of bigotry which seem to me the very essence of the culture Sankaracharya fostered. My vaccinator friend could very well have denounced my suggestion as mere human vanity and lectured to me on the power of faith; but he did not do it, and I believe, could not do it.

*

There is a repose and tranquillity in the air. The river flows softly. Strolling along its edge I notice a group of young men with an elderly companion in their midst. They are all bathing in the river and washing their clothes and are at the same time listening to the lecture their elderly companion is giving them and answering the questions he is putting to them. When they get up to go, muttering their lessons, I follow them through the narrow passage between the consecrated tombs of ancient saints behind Vidyasankara temple.

I follow them into a large hall where groups of students are squatting in shady corners, quietly chanting their lessons and memorizing. A few elderly persons, wrapped in shawls, move about on noiseless feet, absorbed in their own discussion. The place has a monastic quietness.

In the upper storey there is a library containing over four thousand manuscripts and books, neatly classified, labeled and arranged in glass shelves. In an adjoining room some persons are sitting before huge heaps of manuscripts and books; they are at their task of selecting, rejecting, and classifying the vast literary store of manuscripts and books that has accumulated in the *math* from time immemorial. They have been at this task for five years and are likely to go on for a couple of years more.

In the central courtyard there is a shrine, fittingly enough, of Sankaracharya. For this is a college run by the *math*, providing a course of studies which extends over ten years; and here young men are being trained for a religious life. It has about eighty pupils with eight or ten masters, each one an authority in some branch of Sanskrit learning. Forty of the pupils are being looked after by the *math* itself. Once a year the pupils are examined and the passed candidates are led by their masters across the river to the presence of the chief guru, the apostolic head who lives in a house on the opposite bank of the river. He is a man of deep learning and austerity, whose hours are occupied with meditation, prayer, worship and studies. He tests the boys himself, and to those who pass the test he distributes clothes and money gifts.

*

There is a *sanyasi* sweeping the temple of Anjaneya and decorating the image with flowers, completely absorbed in his work, and completely indifferent to those passing him. To my enquiry my guide answers: 'He is one of the four or five *sanyasis* here. He speaks to no one. He came here some years ago and has been here since. We don't know where he has come from. He spends most of his time in yoga: occasionally when he is free he sweeps the temples. Since he is here he is our guest.' I observe two *sanyasis* sitting on the river-step with closed eyes. Their purpose is also unknown. One of them, it was vaguely understood, came all the way from some place in northern India in order to discuss certain questions with the chief guru and have certain doubts cleared. After coming he never met the guru, but just stayed on, dividing his time between meditation and work: he voluntarily teaches certain subjects in the university. There is another *sanyasi* who is here as a pupil in the college. No one questions who they are or why they are here or how long they are going to stay—they are treated as honoured guests as long as they stay. One most noticeable feature of Sringeri is its attitude as host to whoever visits it. The moment you are there you are freed from the concerns of food and shelter. As soon as you get down from the bus you are shown a room in the *dharmashala* or in the guest house. And then your hot water is ready for your bath, and as soon as you have bathed, your food is brought to you. There is an old cook, bent with age, who gets up every morning at four o'clock and goes to bed at eleven in the night, spending his waking hours in serving guests. I saw how deeply the spirit of hospitality had sunk in the people here when I caught the old man in a talkative mood: 'Before I came here I was a clerk in Trichinopoly jail. Through some adverse circumstances I became unhappy, very unhappy and then suffered from mental derangement. I came here, sought the guru, and begged him to permit me to wear the ochre cloth and become a *sanyasi*. He refused because I have a large family to support, and ordered that I should live here with my family and seek peace in serving the pilgrims. And now I have done it for forty years.' He collects the tips given to him, puts them by, and spends it twice a year in feeding the poor. Every day nearly two hundred persons are fed by the *math*, excluding the pupils in the university, the *sanyasis*, and others. This hospitality is not confined to human beings. In the niches of the temple towers there are thousands of pigeons living and breeding. From the stores of the *math* four seers of rice are scattered for the pigeons every day; they provide a grand spectacle when they sweep down for their rice at the feeding hour. In addition to this, five seers of rice are cooked and thrown in the river for the fish. There are numerous fish of all sizes in the river, sporting and splashing about, which come to the surface expectantly whenever any human being stands on the river-step. The fish and the birds have lived and grown without knowing any fear of human beings.

*

There are numerous temples in Sringeri besides the chief one of Sharada. The temple of Vibhandaka in Sringeri itself and of his son Rishyasringa, which is at Kigga, six miles from Sringeri, built on a high hill, are two of the oldest temples here. Both are of the same type with an inner shrine in the middle, an open corridor around, and a roofed platform edging the corridor; the platform can accommodate thousands of persons at a time. It is believed that by praying at these temples rain can be called or stopped. Vibhandaka and his son are famous sages mentioned in the early portions of the *Ramayana*. Rishyasringa, like his father, was a man of great attainment, but he had grown up without seeing a woman. At that time there was a severe drought in Anga; the king was told that the drought would cease if Rishyasringa could be brought to his state and married to the princess. A bevy of young women disguised as hermits were sent in order to entice this sage. They arrived, stopped at Narve, a village near Sringeri, waited for an opportunity and appeared before the young man when his father was out of the scene. He felt such a deep interest in these strange hermits that it was not very difficult for them to decoy him. His approach to Anga brought rain. He married the princess and became the priest of King Dasaratha of Ayodhya, and officiated at the great sacrifice which resulted in the birth of Rama, the hero of the *Ramayana*. There is a carving on a pillar in the Rishyasringa temple at Kigga in which the young sage is shown as he is being carried off happily on a palanquin made of the intertwined arms of fair women.

Another important temple is Vidyasankara's built in about AD 1357. It is on the left bank of Tunga, of Chalukyan style, and built on a raised terrace. Round the outer walls are intricate carvings depicting scenes from the epics and *Puranas*. One of the most interesting figures carved is that of Vyasa discoursing to Sankaracharya. This perhaps illustrates the episode in Sankaracharya's life when the sage Vyasa came to him in the guise of an old man when he was teaching a group of disciples on the banks of Ganges. Sankaracharya was teaching a certain work of which Vyasa himself was the author. Vyasa objected to Sankaracharya's interpretation, and Sankaracharya would not admit the objection. A great debate ensued which went on for seventeen days, neither side giving in. At this the others grew alarmed. Sankaracharya's chief disciple appealed to them: 'Oh, great Vyasa, you are the incarnation of Vishnu, and oh, my master, you are Shiva. When you both argue and debate what is to happen to us, poor mortals? How can we bear to watch this mighty conflict?' And the debate was stopped. Vyasa blessed Sankaracharya for his grasp of the subject and his interpretation. And as Sankaracharya was about to complete his sixteenth year in a couple of hours, Vyasa conferred on him a further span of sixteen years.

The temple of Sharada is the most important institution here. This is the holiest sanctuary which any human being could be privileged to enter, the centre round which the life of Sringeri revolves. At the evening hour of worship the temple is transformed with lights, music, incense and flowers.

Standing at the inner shrine one has a feeling of elation. At this moment the golden image of Sharada in the innermost shrine shining in the lamplight and the swaying flames of camphor, appears to be not a mere metal image but a living presence, and one gets a feeling that one can go on standing here for ever looking at its tranquil and distinguished face.

Kaidala

Gulur village is half-an-hour's journey from Tumkur. Leaving the main road the *jutka* takes an abrupt turn to the right, and a couple of furlongs off we see a small grove in which nestles Kaidala village. At an ancient date it was the capital of a state and known as Kridapura. A comparatively recent and familiar association is the fact that it was the native village of Jakanachari, the famous sculptor. Nriparaya was the ruler of Kridapura when Jakanachari began his career. His travels were extensive since he was engaged now at one court and now at another.

One day when he was at work on an image in the temple at Belur a young man approached him and asked, 'Sir, may I ask you a question?'

'Yes, but don't expect an answer,' said the old sculptor and went on with his work. He was putting the finishing touches on the most important image in the temple—the image of Kesava for whom the temple was being built. The young man asked, 'Is this image intended for worship?'

'Don't stand there and ask foolish questions. You could as well ask if the temple was meant for a god.'

Undaunted by this cynicism the young man declared, 'This image is unfit for worship.'

The old sculptor stood up, shook his mallet at the other, and said 'If you don't leave me instantly I will have you put in chains. Your words are inauspicious and ugly.'

'I can prove that this stone is not pure,' said the young man.

'Can you? See this hand; it has chiseled twenty thousand forms of God till now, but I will chop it off if you will only show me any impurity in this stone.' The young man got a little sandal paste and smeared it over the figure. The paste dried everywhere except near the navel, where, on examination, was found a cavity containing a toad.

The image was set aside as being unfit for worship, and Jakanachari cut off his arm according to his vow. It was later found that the critic was none other than his son out in search of a long-lost father. After this Jakanachari was directed in a dream to return to his village and build a temple for

Kesava. He obeyed the vision. When he completed the temple his arm was restored to him. *Kai Dala* means the restored arm. This temple can be seen even today. Some idea of its date is given by an inscription in the adjacent Iswara temple which was also built by Jakanachari. The inscription records that the temples were built in about AD 1150 in the reign of the Hoysala king, Narasimha.

Devaraya Durga

About nine miles from Tumkur, a fortified hill. Behind a forest bungalow at the foot of the hill there is a very attractive spot called Namada Chilme— a little cavity in a rocky bed, a cubit deep, from which wells up an inexhaustible supply of water. This cavity, no bigger than a brass utensil, fills up as often as the water is removed, and it supplies all the water needed for gardening, bathing and washing hereabouts. It is said that in the evenings peacocks, which are in plenty here, come out and dance around this spring. The place owes its name to the legend that Rama, while on his expedition to Lanka, stopped here. He needed a little water for mixing his *nama* (forehead marking) and made this cavity in the rock. At his divine touch even a stone yielded water.

The summit of Devaraya Durga is 4,000 feet above sea level. The road winds up through thick jungles. On the summit there is a temple dedicated to Narasimhaswami, and there is another temple for the same god in the village 800 feet below.

Mysore City

Mysore was once the royal capital; when it ceased to be that, it became the Governor's residence, but later it ceased to be even that when the Governor's office was moved to Bangalore. Long before the All India Radio was thought of, Akashvani had its birth in the Vontikoppal Extension of Mysore, and then the All India Radio came along, absorbed it, and moved off to Bangalore, abandoning a perfectly designed studio. Mysore was the seat of the University, but after the creation of a Bangalore University its jurisdiction has shrunk. All things that could be dislodged and shifted have been moved from Mysore. What has been left behind is the Chamundi hill with its temple, also the rivers Kaveri and Kabini on the outskirts and the forests on the farther perimeter with their tigers, bisons, elephants, and a hundred other creatures. To me at any rate, the really worthwhile things are still here, and form an immutable background to life in Mysore, which goes on unruffled, free from the fret and fury of modern city life. The railway offices and workshop, the silk, sandal oil and scooter factories, and the Krishnarajendra Mills, where the maximum number of persons are employed, receive their workers and release them at the end of the day without creating any obvious rush or peak-hour scenes.

The pedestrian still commands mastery of the roads; the next, in order of priority, are cycles in a kind of mobile barricade, while the riders of bullock carts with fuel from the jungles always appear deeply absorbed in sorting out their problems, then *tongas*, which in consideration of the state of their horses, are permitted at will as long as they hurt no one. I am saying nothing about autorickshaws because Mysore has the unique distinction of having only one of its kind.* Cattle, singly or in herd, moving, recumbent or stationary hold top priority in all the public thoroughfares; especially buffaloes which enjoy a privileged existence (in spite of the fact that the Goddess on the hills incarnated herself especially to destroy the buffalo demon Mahisha). When all these items of traffic have passed automobiles,

* This is no longer the case. Mysore now has a large number of these indispensable vehicles.

trucks and lorries, get their clearance. It's challenging: if one can drive in Mysore, one can drive anywhere in the world.

A visitor to the city once asked why the bulk of the population of Mysore city, mostly in groups of four or six, seemed to be concentrated in its streets. The answer is simple. Mysoreans have not yet lost the use of their limbs; the distances are not insuperable, and the weather and the general surroundings are always conducive to a walking philosophy, tempting one to go out. A day's visit to the 'market side' is indispensable, if not actually for shopping at least to meet people. As in ancient Athens, people settle many matters of philosophy, politics and personal affairs, while promenading around the statue or strolling down Sayaji Rao Road. But this creates certain traffic problems as such discussions, by preference, are held on road junctions, rather than on the very broad footpaths (which, for mysterious reasons, are detested and avoided by one and all).

Driving in Mysore is peculiarly complicated as one must be able to weave one's way without losing one's serenity of mind. If the accident-statistics of Mysore are negligible it is not for want of opportunities, but it is due to the general all-round good humour, and a certain imperviousness in the Mysore temperament; no driver ever would dream of demanding the right of way and the pedestrian has confidence and knows that it will not be necessary for him to interrupt his conversation and move, as the vehicle, if need arises, could always move on to the footpath which is just there waiting to be used.

Mysore has not much excitement to offer: a couple of clubs, an annual music season lasting for a fortnight, the Dasara festivities, a few university functions or lectures, are all the events that a citizen can look forward to, but life in general possesses a quiet beneath the surface intensity, imparted to it by the natural surroundings. However, the noteworthy seasonal transformations, the grand pyrotechnical lighting that rends the pitch-black skies of summer storms, falls of hail, the fleecy clouds floating across the lit-up tower of the Chamundi hill temple, and the absolutely unmatched sunsets over Kukkana Halli tank touching up the hill with iridescence, are matters of moment for us; one notices, enjoys, and talks about them. I have said nothing about the trees of Mysore yet. Mysore has probably the most versatile collection of trees (estimated to be about ten thousand) of any city in the world. I have heard persons in far off countries refer to the Gold Mohur season of Mysore, when a whole road is canopied with orange and red blooms, to be followed by purple Jacaranda here and there, or absolutely flaming-red Spathodia; in Mysore one finds the Padri flower, that extraordinary, delicate-scented flower which blooms for only a week in a year in March. Mysore has flowers or foliage to offer all round the year, but unfortunately one gets so used to one's gifts that one takes them for granted; in other countries or even other Indian cities one would have guarded and trained them with all the might of local authority; but here foliage and flowers are broken off by the lorryload in the event of marriages or even in connection with a ministerial visit (as I found out once). Occasionally the elephant from the stables just breaks off a tree for its breakfast: I once remember an irate officer marching off an elephant with the mahout to the Laxmipuram police station; but that was years ago, nowadays no one minds it; the authorities are totally indifferent or plead helplessness, and the average citizen does not interfere. I worry over this problem as much as one worries about possible nuclear disasters. I spoke to a municipal authority on this subject once: he thanked me for drawing his attention to the subject, rang up his assistant and asked him to look up the by-laws and immediately tell him how it could be prevented; the assistant said 'Yes, sir,' and there the matter rests; that was over a year ago.

This is the sad part of it today—a feeling one gets that Mysore has been abandoned by its guardians. Garbage heaps keep growing by the roadside; tenemental constructions proliferate over carefully planned old extensions; the streets look sinister at nightfall, are ill-lit or not lit at all in most places (Mysore was called a city of lights once); roads are pitted in most areas, with potholes camouflaged with pebbles and a smearing of tar (a highly individual technique evolved by our road-makers on the basis 'out of sight, out of mind'); and above all we had the finest filtered water supply once upon a time. Now one hears with shock that it's only half-filtered. The man who mentioned it asked, 'Isn't it better than nothing?' How can it be? It is in the same category as poison or sin, for there can be no such thing as semi-sinfulness or semi-poison; I hear rumours that finances are being found for a hundred per cent filtering of water. I hope it will be done before there is one more attack of cholera.

The House I Built

The other day I was asked by a friend, 'When did you acquire this suntan?' I didn't know that I had. We are endowed by nature with a complexion that is predisposed to a suntan even without the sun. I don't think that anyone would notice such a thing in our country; but here, perhaps, it was a very marked condition—my original complexion must have turned several shades deeper. I remembered the cause in a flash. I was building a house—an occupation enough to turn milk-white skin to brown, brown into dark, and probably dark into white again! Young people grow old in the process, and mild natures become fierce. Building a house is no ordinary or comfortable experience. Yet why does one seek it? Not voluntarily, of course. Here is its history.

It was said in former times: 'Fools build houses for wise men to live in!' Whenever one thinks of house-building it's inevitable this saying should cross one's mind. Unfortunately its sense has not been deeply examined. I suspect that this saying has been invented and popularized by a set of perpetual tenants . . . a sort of fraternity cry. I don't think one would dare to say it before one's house-owner. Mark I say 'house-owner'. I prefer this word to the other excessively flattering term 'landlord'. We don't say 'taxi-lord', or 'hotel-lord' of persons who live by hiring out something; why do we say 'landlord'? I think it has been coined as a piece of flattery, something to please a man who owned a house so that he might be prevailed upon to let it; and after getting the house, the tenant chuckled within himself and said, 'Fools build houses for wise men to live in!'

I used to say so myself, while I remained a tenant in a certain house for fourteen years. I thought I was a very wise man. No worry, no labour; you just walked in and occupied it, and when you wanted even a small area of plaster to be repaired, you called up the man who took the rent and asked him to attend to it, and watched with detachment while he struggled with masons and whitewashers. If the other did not carry out your wishes you said pugnacious things such as that you would move on to another house, much nicer and cheaper, in the same street, and that you had been staying here all these days only in order to help the man and so forth. You might assume as lofty a tone as you liked and yet you would never be in danger of finding yourself and all your baggage in the street in front of the house.

That was a golden age. But, as any historian will tell you, time is fickle; the golden age is short-lived and only a prelude to the dark age. The golden age for habitual tenants ended sometime during the Second World War. It was marked by the house-owner suddenly telling his old tenant one fine day, 'Please vacate the house next month.'

This was a bombshell. It was as if someone had asked you to vacate your own body and go elsewhere. It seemed impossible, inconceivable, that you should go and live anywhere else. In spite of all your bluster before the other you could never dream of going to another house and calling it your home. This was more or less built to your needs: that side room for guests, that top room for the brother from Bombay whenever he came, and the front hall and the veranda; the view of the *margosa* tree from your veranda (you grew up with the tree), and then those little creepers beside the front window. This house was part and parcel of yourself: you knew it intimately, every inch; you knew which spot under the roof would leak in mild rain and which during a downpour; you knew where the afternoon sun would attack you, and you knew a place in the passage which could be treated as Ooty in the summer; you knew where the full moon would steal in, and also which part of the house was vulnerable to a burglar's entry .... You knew all this and also loved the tall, gawky citrus plant which put forth a single, hard-skinned, cadaverous fruit after nearly ten years of tending. You watered the citrus all your spare hours and never let any child go near it.

You feel desolate at the thought of going away from it all. 'No. Impossible. I can't leave this house . . .'

But suddenly you realize that your house-owner, who used to be such a sweet and amiable man, has suddenly assumed the features of a demon. You see a hard resoluteness in his eyes. You ask, 'Why do you want us to vacate?'

'We want to come and live in this house ourselves.'

'You have a house already . . .'

'Yes, but we want to pull it down and rebuild it.'

You don't quite appreciate this move and say something and then the landlord opens a second front: 'We want this house in any case for the sake of my mother's health.'

'What is the matter with your mother's health?' you ask, detecting concern in the other for his mother for the first time.

'She is very weak, and doctors have advised a change.'

'They're right,' you say. 'Go for a change. Why don't you take her to Kodaikanal?'

'Not that sort of change. . . . They want us to change only the house. Too much noise in that street.'

'Why don't you give her vitamin complex?' you suggest solicitously.

'We are giving her that. Please vacate the house by the first of next month.'

The first of next month turns up. You don't vacate. You also have an elderly person at home for whose well-being you are entitled to show consideration: there is something wrong with her. Your doctor has advised that you should not disturb her. Now the owner of the house gets his turn to make solicitous enquiries and offer suggestions about vitamin complex, and you listen to all his advice and then say, 'Thank you, but the most important thing is that she should not be disturbed.'

'What exactly is the matter with her?' he asks.

'Just a general weakness,' you say. 'You see in matters affecting the health of elderly persons, we cannot be too careful.'

This gives you a couple of months more; and then perhaps an expectant mother . . . (even a stout-hearted house-owner stands helpless before this reason), and then the tribulations of a new-born infant. The house-owner has to watch anxiously over the growth of the child, for he can get the house only if the baby is in a fit condition to be moved out. And then possibly you can add a month more because of the stars or almanac. One or the other, all human reasons which no landlord (by the way, there seems to be no escape from this word) can brush aside; however, the one real reason all the time being that you cannot find another house because you look for a replica of this house with all its surroundings, even down to such a last detail as the one-fruit-yielding citrus plant.

It is a trial of patience between you and the landlord; and when considerable time has elapsed the landlord accepts defeat by agreeing to your staying on for six months more provided you agree to an enhancement of rent. You haggle over the exact figure and strike a bargain, and he lets you stay on—strictly for six months; at the end of this period you must vacate. You readily agree, and in your relief add, 'I will vacate even earlier if I get a good house,' and you decide to be on the lookout. Six months seem such a long time.

Six months pass too swiftly and you are back where you were. During this phase all the suavity of manners are gone. Desperation has given an edge to your landlord's tone. He is no longer prepared to show an interest in your family welfare. His tone becomes more and more aggressive each day. You go on repeating that surely he doesn't expect you to move to a *chatram* with all the children and baggage, and that you are only too eager to move on provided another house is available. You wouldn't care to stay on a moment longer than necessary. This reasonable attitude does not impress the other. He is definitely unpleasant. You are losing nerve. Every day you dread his footsteps on the veranda; and you come to the stage of looking sullen and treating him as an enemy. You consult a lawyer friend on your position; your rights and liabilities under the provisions of the Rent Control Act. This sort of living cannot go on forever; it suddenly dawns on you that the whole system of living is barbaric: the continuous tension, evasion, falsehood and prevarication are unworthy of a civilized existence.

The whole thing, the whole demoralization and barbarity, is due to the want of a house of one's own. A house, like clothes or food, is a primary and basic need for every human being. You wouldn't wear rented clothes all your life, would you? It is utter degradation to be living in another man's house, and expecting to spend a lifetime there. When your mind has set itself going on these lines, you quiver with excitement; you feel that you have made a sudden discovery in life. A hundred reasons occur to you now as to why you should have a house of your own. It doesn't seem to matter where you get the land for it and how you build. . . . You can add or subtract as much as you like from it; your favourite corners will always remain yours; you can grow a wonderful garden; you can do what you like with the place, and above all, you won't have to pay rent every month . . . All the usual arguments that occur to everybody under the sun, now sound very novel and original to you in your present state of mind.

You are so intoxicated that you feel like turning up your nose at the landlord the next time he comes. You no longer dread his arrival as before. He is just another human being, that is all. You are neither repulsed nor attracted by him. He is just a visitor, that is all. You make him wait and then come out.

He is waiting to ask the stock question, 'When are you going to vacate?' You look bored. The thought of building a house has given you a new confidence and assurance of manner and the house-owner looks somewhat tamed by it. You answer casually, 'Well, I am going to vacate it, don't worry. I am anxious to vacate as much as you, if not more. I am moving into a house of my own.'

This acts as a spell on the other. All his old affability seems to return. He feels that you are of his class. You are no longer a member of the enemy. Now he seems to feel that he can allow you to remain here as long as you like. All his old aggressiveness is gone. He is actually interested in your proposed house as if it were his own. He says, 'Oh, building a house! Oh, what a bother these days! Building a house is no joke these days.' You feel you are being looked upon as a hero. You say casually, 'I hope you won't start bothering me to leave . . .' 'Oh, no,' he says. 'If your house is coming up where is the point in shifting and putting yourself to all the trouble . . . I mean, I don't like to put people to unnecessary trouble. My principle always is not to trouble tenants unnecessarily,' and suggests at the end of the interview a further rise in rent for the duration of your stay. You contest it hotly at first. But it is no use. He appeals to you as a friend, as an old friend. You wonder if you could take up the matter with the Rent Controller but the other tells you a story of a tenant who appealed to the Rent Controller against a rise. The tenant had been paying a hundred rupees, and the owner suddenly wanted one hundred and fifty. The man appealed to the Rent Controller who inspected the house and fixed the fair rent at two hundred and twenty, much to the chagrin of the tenant. The tenant took up the case further and appealed to the next authority, who inspected the house and fixed the rent at three hundred and twenty-five rupees. There being no other authority of appeal and there being no other house available, the man had no option but to pay. . . He now sweated and earned just enough to pay his monthly rent. . . At the end of the story you say, 'Oh, no, these are things we must settle as between friends, there is no point in dragging such small matters before the authorities whatever may be the merit of the case,' strengthened more than ever in your resolve to try and build a *house of your own* (a hypnotic phrase this).

And one fine day you take a jump into the unknown sea, and pass directly into a world of new facts and values.

The Indian Theatre

The entire village is in great excitement. All normal work is suspended. In the *maidan* hectic activity is going on. Hundreds of youngsters are moving hither and thither. Children are rolling on the ground and screaming in sheer joy. The men are extremely busy. They are building a stage. Wooden planks, bamboo matting, coconut *thaties* are brought in large and scattered quantities. Everyone is bringing up whatever he can supply: the *dhobi* of the village, for instance, is bringing numerous sheets and pieces of coloured cloth with which to drape the stage. The costumes are provided by the village folk themselves and everyone is happy that something that he can give is going to be useful for the drama. The carpenter of the village has taken the responsibility of supplying all the planks and poles necessary for the erection of the stage. The goldsmith appears to be the art director of the whole show: he is bringing in tinsel and brocade and has assumed the responsibility for costumes and ornaments. There is also the village schoolmaster who normally seats the young boys of the village on the *pyol* of his house and teaches them reading and writing. Today he is directing the drama: he creates the dialogues and the songs, and trains all the actors. The drama is not written down, but improvized in one or two rehearsals. The village barber, whose traditional side-occupation is playing on pipes and drums, is responsible for all the music; he and the village tom-tom beater provide, between them, all the sound and musical effects required for the play. The barber plays his pipe when the music is to be soft and gentle as when the hero and the heroine are heralded on the stage, and the other beats the tom-tom fiercely when some *rakshasa* or a noisy extrovert character like Bhima appears. By evening the stage is ready: coconut fronds and banana stalks are tied up at the portals of the stage as an auspicious decoration.

The stage is illuminated with torches and flares soaked in oil given by the oil-monger, and the ground is swept and water-sprinkled. The play starts at about ten or even later. Before that the organizers go around with pipe and drum and garlands to invite all the important citizens of the village. This is a courtesy which has to be strictly observed with proper codes of precedence, etc., and special carpets supplied by one of the distinguished patrons themselves are spread for the elect in the front row. The rest of the audience seat themselves wherever they like.

There are certain formalities which are strictly observed in presenting a play: the *sutradhara*, most likely the schoolmaster himself with his face painted and wearing a cloak and turban, enters and offers his salutation to the distinguished gathering, and then he tells them what tale they are about to see and explains its import. The story is usually a well-known episode from the *Ramayana* or the *Mahabharata* or the *Bhagavata*, those store-houses of dramatic material. All his speech is rhythmic, ornate and musical, and it is more than likely the sound instrument keeps time when he is speaking. The story opens. There is no such thing as a curtain going up. The village stage has no drop curtain. The characters arrive and depart in full view of the audience, and nobody minds. The 'Green Room' is a little away from the stage, and it enables the characters to arrive on the stage in proper style and tempo. The 'tom-tom beaters drum up a great tempo when a turbulent character takes the stage, and he enters with the maximum noise and swagger. Every character has to dance. In fact there is no drama without music or dance. All the characters have to perform their roles not only through their facial expressions and lines, but also through their dances—the music being soft or vigorous. There are certain conventions even regarding paint and makeup: deeper shades and multi-colour effects are reserved for those who are expected to strike revulsion or terror into the hearts of the onlookers. Lighter shades are all reserved for good and agreeable characters. And the roles of women are always played by men disguised.

At dawn, when the light is seen in the east, they sing *mangalam* and close the play. Though it has gone on for six hours continuously, nobody has felt bored. The flares of the torches, the glittering garments, the beat of the drums, and the music have kept the audience in a spell and they are really sorry that the enchantment is over.

India's half-a-million villages derive their dramatic entertainment from theatrical groups like the one described above, and these are to be found, if not in each village, then at least in each group of villages. In addition to this there are itinerant marionette players and 'shadow' players. The shadow show is performed with semi-transparent leather cut-out figures which are brightly painted; a thin white curtain hangs down before the audience. The cut-out figures are held before kerosene lamps, appro-priate dialogue or songs being 'voiced' by the various persons behind the curtain, who manipulate the figures. They present mythological episodes generally, and often succeed in producing highly dramatic effects. This kind of company is able to carry its entire equipment in a basket and generally moves about in search of crowded fairs and festivals.

Kathakali, a feature of Malabar, is a world-famous mode, producing dramatic effects through dance, gestures and expressions. Yakshagana, a very popular feature of Konkan, presents its episodes through the dialogues spoken by one group of persons while all the movement and acting is done by a separate group, with perfect synchronization between the two. Harikatha performances, though strictly not in the theatrical category, are intensely dramatic. One man, with music and narration, presents a story. This is peculiar to this country, and may be roughly described as mono-acting with musical accompaniments. It depends not so much on setting as on the musical and narrative abilities of one single individual. The theatrical tradition in this country in fact values extreme simplicity of setting and costume. In ancient times the classical Sanskrit dramas were performed in front of a single drop and it was the poetic force of a composition that produced the illusions. It was not necessary to bring on the stage elaborate realistic apparatus. If King Dusyanta came looking for a gazelle it was not necessary to drive a live animal across the stage: the actor by his expression and movement conveyed the effect, aided by the speech of the *sutradhara* who usually filled up gaps and supplied the links in the story. The *sutradhara* is still a part and parcel of every drama as is also the *vidushaka*, or the clown, who continuously lightens the situations with his remarks and innuendoes. Seeing these we have a feeling that the tradition of centuries still runs through the whole activity, though in a subdued form.

It was feared at one time that the rise of cinema would adversely affect the theatre. To a certain extent it did, but of late there has been a tremendous revival in dramatic art.

The Cold Fruit

One of the most troublesome problems of research scholars is fixing the date of Avvaiyar, the Tamil poetess. I suppose it is outrageous to suggest that her date may be fixed any time between the tenth century BC and fifteenth century AD. I beg the forgiveness of scholars for my wild and inexact conjecture, but my feeling is that when the right date is so much in dispute there is nothing wrong in giving any date. After going through some research material I have come to the conclusion, a somewhat broad one, that Avvaiyar existed sometime within the last ten thousand years. And when this is accepted there arises a further problem as to whether there has been only one person of that name or many, and a further controversy as to who is the genuine one among them, and which of such and such an epigram could be attributed to the real Avvaiyar and which to the bogus ones. I fear that we are likely to lose sight of our main subject when we get into such a wilderness of research and scholarship, particularly when we find that every scholar is completely convincing and speaks with the utmost authority.

Avvaiyar as a concept is readily accepted by everyone and I think that is enough for our purpose. She is generally pictured as carrying a bundle of palm-leaf writings slung over her back, staff in one hand, bent with years, and trudging the highway. The entire Tamil Nadu was her home, the blue sky over the highway was her roof. She walked into the courts of kings and walked out of them as she liked. She spoke with the same kindliness and irony to a king as to a woodcutter, and accepted their hospitality on her own terms. Her writings range from the simplest alphabet book, which children recite even today, to the highest class of literary composition. Wherever she went she helped people acquire a balanced outlook and an awareness of eternal values. Her intellectual and spiritual integrity was of the highest order. Her tongue uttered freely what her mind felt to be the truth, and there was no one who could contradict her or teach her anything. Her eminence was assured and accepted not only by kings and commoners but also by all the poets and scholars of her day. This is a dangerous phase in the career of any intellectual: a certain smugness and a subtle kind of arrogance inevitably develop in one who attains this height. God, as Avvaiyar felt, saved her in time from falling into this error.

During one of her wanderings she came to rest one warm afternoon under the shade of a *jumbu* tree. She leaned on the tree-trunk, relaxed her limbs, and shut her eyes. Just then a voice called, 'Granny, are you asleep?' Avvaiyar looked up and saw a radiant urchin sitting on a high branch and grinning at her.

'Who are you, little man? What do you want?' she asked.

'You see there? All those are my cows. I am watching them.'

'Sitting so high?' she asked.

'Yes, I have to be here. Otherwise I can't see all my flock, which are grazing up to that horizon and beyond.'

Avvaiyar laughed at this conceit. 'So many cows! All of them yours?' she asked.

'Yes, all that and more that are not seen. . . . Moreover this tree is full of likeable fruits. I can be both eating and watching here. Do you want some? Shall I shake a branch for you?'

'Very well, if it will please you,' said Avvaiyar. 'Just one or two will do for me.'

The boy asked now, 'Do you want it hot or cold?'

Avvaiyar felt puzzled, 'What do you mean?'

The boy replied earnestly, 'I want to know whether you want your fruit hot or cold? Don't you know the meaning of hot and cold?'

'Yes, I do, but what is a hot fruit on a tree?'

'Oh, granny!' the boy exclaimed, 'You look so wise and learned, can't you understand this simple thing?'

The old lady racked her mind to understand what this precocious youngster might mean. She had never felt so bewildered in her life.

The boy pursued her relentlessly, 'Granny, why are you so silent? What a long time you take to say whether you want your fruit hot or cold.'

In order to get over the situation quickly, Avvaiyar replied, 'Give me a couple of fruits and let them be cold; I am too old to like them hot.'

The boy shook the branch on which he was sitting, and a few purple fruits fell on the sandy ground.

Avvaiyar picked up one and, before putting it into her mouth, blew away a few particles of sand sticking on the fruit.

'Stop! Stop!' cried the urchin. 'Is that fruit so hot that you have to blow on it? You should have caught it in your saree-end if you wanted it cold.'

Now the meaning of the urchin's phrase dawned on her. She looked up at the boy in admiration. The boy smiled at her. She saw him suddenly as an incarnation of God Subramanya himself. She burst into a song praising His Grace.

The boy merely replied, 'You are saying all sorts of things, granny, do you want some more fruit?'

'No, no, one fruit has given me enough lesson. . .'

'Granny, I will ask you a question. Will you answer it?'

'I will try,' replied Avvaiyar with trepidation, wondering if he was going to lay a trap for her again.

'Which is bigger than the biggest?' asked the boy.

Avvaiyar recited a song:

> *The universe is the biggest*
> *Bigger than that is the Four-Faced Brahma*
> *Brahma's support is Vishnu*
> *Vishnu rests on the wavy ocean*
> *The wavy ocean is but a little*
> *water on the palm of the microcosmic sage Agastya*
> *Agastya came out of a pot*
> *The pot is but a handful of mud out of the earth*
> *The Earth is just a load on one of the thousand heads of the*
> * mighty snake*
> *The mighty snake is a ring adorning the little*
> * finger of Parvathi*
> *Parvathi is just a half of her spouse Shiva*
> *who resides in the heart of a true devotee*
> *Is there anything to measure the expanse*
> *of a devotee's heart?*

The boy said, 'You seem to be very learned, granny.'

Avvaiyar replied, 'It is my unique fortune to hear that compliment from your lips.' She made her obeisance to him.

The boy said, 'You may go your way now, granny. Don't forget me.' 'Who can ever forget you?' replied Avvaiyar as she started on her onward journey.

The Mirror (An Ancient Tale)

Thousands of years ago a peasant and his wife were living happily—a tranquil and undisturbed existence full of understanding and harmony—till a wayfarer presented the husband with a small square looking glass and went his way. The glass had been tucked away in a leather pouch. The wayfarer gave it with the advice, 'Never take it out of the pouch.'

'Then why should I keep it?'

'It is a talisman which will do you a lot of good as long as you don't look at it. Beware! On the day you pull it out, you will lose your peace of mind.'

The peasant took it home and secreted it in a corner of the family trunk. But in a moment of impulse, he confessed to his wife, 'I have something you must not know about.' Why he should have said precisely the thing that would upset and intrigue a wife cannot be easily explained.

She asked coolly, 'Why not?'

'I don't know why, but you must not go near it. It is not fit for women,' which answer stimulated her interest further. She merely exclaimed, 'Oh, I see. . . I will bear it in mind.' She pretended not to be interested in it and put him off the scent. Next day when he was away at the fields, she gently opened the box, and took out the pouch with trembling hands. She sent out a silent prayer to the gods to forgive her, 'Oh gods! You will agree with me that a husband should have no secrets from his wife. . .' She quietly pulled the looking glass out of its pouch and at first saw only the blank side, and exclaimed, 'Pooh! Is this all? I don't know why he made all this fuss about it. Men have a habit of making a lot of fuss about trivial things.' As she was about to slip it back into the pouch she felt with her finger that the other side was excessively smooth, turned it over and uttered a scream. Her husband had been treasuring the portrait of some woman! She was appalled at the depth of his cunning. In her rage she gnashed her teeth, and the other also did it. 'Oh, a witch's portrait!' the wife exclaimed. 'It is only a witch's portrait that is known to make faces at the person that beholds it!' she cried. She quietly put it back in the trunk and never breathed a word of what she had done to anybody. She watched her husband's movements more closely. It only confirmed her suspicion. She found that he was suffering from some very deep preoccupation. He smiled, spoke, ate, and moved about, but it was evident that his thoughts were elsewhere. The wife pretended to be going out to a friend's house, came round by the back door and observed the man from a dark unseen corner. The man was seen to hover about the family trunk with a song on his lips, perform worshipful gestures in front of it, and what is more light an incense stick for it. This was too much for the wife. She rushed out with a cry of rage. The husband was knocked down by the force of the impact. She attacked him with her claws crying, 'Oh, you darling of the witches!' He extricated himself from her hold, overpowered her and locked her up in a room. She went on raving inside much to the distress of this man. He thought that this was time to put the talisman to some good use. If he could somehow introduce it into her room without her knowledge, it might work its spell on her and relieve her. He reverently took out the pouch, pressed it to his eyes, and prayed, 'Please help my wife recover her wits, poor creature!' When he held the pouch in his hand, he was overwhelmed with curiosity. He threw all caution to the winds and took out the contents of the pouch. He let out a shout of rage. Here was the portrait of a man. He gnashed his teeth, and the other too followed his example. Who was this grinning magician whose portrait he had been cherishing in his house all along? Only the portrait of a magician could grin and make faces. Could it be...? He tried to suppress the thought, but there it was. Could it be that the portrait was a memento meant for his wife? Could it be a conspiracy between his wife and her admirer to fool him? Now thinking it over, every little action of his wife's seemed to be significant. She had been behaving in a most sinister and suspicious manner. She had pretended not to be interested in the 'talisman', otherwise what a lot of questions she would have normally put to him! He understood now why she had pounced upon him when he approached the family trunk.

He felt so angry at this trickery that he smashed the glass on the ground, stamped on it, and threw it into the gutter, which carried it away immediately out of sight. The wife's condition improved after this since she took the gesture on the part of her husband as proof that he had got over a passing fancy. The husband was pleased with the improvement he noticed in his wife and graciously overlooked the temporary lapse she had displayed. Peace reigned in that household again, with a tacit understanding between the partners that there should be no more mention of the bewitching portrait.

As we advance in years we look less and less into a mirror; therein lies peace of mind. No adult uses a mirror except for taking a hurried glance at his chin. We prefer, as we grow older, not to have a too detailed view of ourselves. Anyone who catches a sudden glimpse of himself in a full-size mirror cannot help feeling a slight shock. 'Oh, is this how I look!' he exclaims to himself unless he is afflicted with the Narcissus complex. Narcissus, according to Greek mythology, was a youth who fell in love with his reflection in the water and was drowned.

Musical Commerce

We came out of the Music Sabha, loudly discussing the state of present-day music. The Talkative Man, whom we had thought we had shaken off unobtrusively earlier in the day, said: 'Commercialism? You think music is too much commercialized today? Well, listen now. I don't think even your worst experience can match mine.' This is his story:

I once knew a very great musician called Saravana Bhagavathar. He was a genius if ever there was one. I don't know how many of you have heard about him—a venerable man with a gold bead at his throat, living on his ancestral lands, and coming of a long line of singers. He never thought that he needed anything more in life than to be left alone to sing. No publicity, no bank books, no crowded concerts, no idea of having anything to do with a public—just being left alone to sing, clasping his *thambura*. He was a man of such self-content that it was very difficult to get him out to sing anywhere. If anyone wanted to hear him he would have to go to his house and stay on as his guest. There was no knowing when he would start singing or stop if he started. People just hung about all over the place, and when they saw him reaching out for his *thambura*, they gathered around him. Sometimes he took up a *raga* and worked it up so elaborately that he would sing it for a whole week, with the briefest possible interruption for food or sleep.

Such people ought to be left alone. But there are vain men who just won't allow that. They take a special delight in pulling a man like that out of his shelter and corrupting him. Such a man was my friend Balram. He was a prominent businessman, Chamber of Commerce President and all that, and he normally lived in glittering style. Adding to it came the wedding of his daughter with the commercial prince of another district, fixed for the coming month. Balram wanted to do something outstanding, or rather everything outstanding, on this occasion. He had engaged the most gaudily-dressed drummers and bandsmen to be in attendance, he had a couch constructed out of strings of jasmine and tinsel, shaped like a Dakota, to seat the bridal pair during the reception and he had made all the attendants around it dress like pilots, and he hit upon the idea of asking Saravana Bhagavathar to sing during the reception. It was not because he was enamoured of his music. He wanted to engage him because he had heard that no one else had succeeded in drawing the old gentleman out. He knew that I was very friendly with the old gentleman and ordered me to procure his services: 'I want none but Saravana Bhagavathar to sing for Saroja's wedding. She will remember it with pride all her life. If she likes it, I'm even prepared to engage him to teach her music. I will buy the instrument he plays on. What is that instrument?'

'No instrument,' I said. 'He is a vocal musician.'

'Oh!' he said lightly, though rather disappointed.

'All right, let him teach her vocal music.' He added after a little rumination, 'Well, all that for a later occasion. For the present, fetch him for the reception no matter at what price.' I had feared it might prove difficult to persuade the old gentleman to sing at the wedding, but luckily for me chance had made my task unexpectedly easier: when I saw him next I found him engaged in tackling the problem of an interest amount due on a mortgage. He was in urgent need of finding a thousand odd rupees immediately. When I offered him four hundred rupees for Balram's engagement, suggesting that it would pay part of the interest, he was mightily pleased and relieved.

Balram's invitation proclaimed in golden letters: 'Reception 6 p.m.— Music by Sri Saravana Bhagavathar, who has never sung in public before. A unique occasion.'

A gorgeous dais was raised facing the bridal Dakota. The old musician sat on it clasping his *thambura*. Balram, who watched this with gratification, said: 'You told me he didn't play on any instrument. He is playing on one now!' I explained to him as casually as I could that the *thambura* was only an accompanying 'drone' and not an instrument to play on.

The hall was filled to overcrowding. The old gentleman showed the utmost indifference to the gathering. He shut his eyes tight and hummed a single note for about twenty minutes to see if his voice was in unison with the pitch of the accompanying instruments. One feared he had fallen into a trance, his eyes shut, his voice emitting a continuous long sound like a bumble-bee flying at the rafters. After this, he opened his eyes, looked about and uttered *Sa Pa Sa* in three octaves, each lasting about fifteen minutes. To Balram it was all the same. He had stuffed himself into a dark tweed suit, and was busily engaged in smiling at his distinguished visitors, shaking their hands, and leading them on to the Dakota so that they might shake hands with his son-in-law too.

It was about nine o'clock when Saravana Bhagavathar came out of his preliminary voice testing and started on a note resembling *Thodi raga*. It was ten o'clock when he completed a particular song—the first full song for the whole evening. It was an admirable execution, no doubt, but the hall was required for other purposes. A dinner had been arranged and hungry and expectant guests had already arrived wearing shirts and with towels over their shoulders: not all the guests invited for the music were included in the dinner list, and it was imperative that the music should stop and the hall be cleared. Secondly, there was some religious function also to be gone through by the bride and bridegroom and the priests were standing around the hall sullenly. The hall was crammed with people who were lost in the music. They seemed to have forgotten where they were or why they were there. Gradually the cooks, a dozen of them, came out of the kitchen and stood on the fringe of the gathering with gloomy and angry faces. The master of the house called me aside and said: 'This music *must* stop. The cooks are threatening to walk out if the dinner is delayed. The hall must be cleared at once.' I looked about: the cooks certainly looked resolute and grim, the guests were beginning to look famished, women and children drooped, half asleep, the master of the house and his adjutants moved about with suppressed excitement while the musician sang inspiredly, and his admirers sat transfixed.

It was nearing midnight. The master of the house was reluctant to create a scene though his fretfulness had increased. I waited for an opportunity, crawled up on the dais behind the musician, and when he paused for breath whispered: 'I think you can sing the *mangalam* now.' He just glared at me, cleared his throat, and began a rather elaborate *alapana* in *Kalyani*.

I was panic-stricken. It was his favourite *raga*, and he might sing it for a whole week, and all the dinner guests might be dead by that time. The worst of it all was that the bridegroom himself was an inordinate music-lover, and would not get up till the music stopped. Otherwise it would have been the easiest thing to close the music by asking the priests to chant aloud their *mantras*, and the cooks to spread out dining leaves wherever space was available, completely ignoring the musician. We had to move very cautiously in this matter, and stop the music in a seemingly natural manner. The accompanying players presented a pathetic spectacle. The violinist was just scraping the strings feebly and the drummer's palms had evidently begun to bleed; their shoulders drooped and their faces were woebegone.

The situation seemed hopeless. The master of the house signalled to me from behind the bridegroom's seat (he was presumably suggesting to him to get up). He indicated with his fingers one and two cyphers and waved up. I understood and whispered to the musician, when he took a breath half-way through *Kalyani*: 'He will pay you a bonus of fifty rupees more if you will stop the performance immediately.' He paused and looked at me with a smile. I thought I had won. But he continued *Kalyani*. Close upon its heel he began a song in *Sahana*. The accompanists gave up all pretences to following him. They just hugged their instruments and blinked unhappily.

The master of the house ran about the hall like a scorpion-stung rabbit. If he had not been checked by his son-in-law's enthusiasm for music, he would have gagged and thrown out the singer. He threw helpless looks at me as I sat behind the musician, and sent me another signal. Before *Sahana* was over, the musician's fee had been raised to five hundred. He bit his lips, smiled, and threw me a cunning look. I never knew he was such a mercenary. He was clearly working up to the highest possible bid. He sang without a pause—one song following another closely, not giving me an opportunity to put in a word edge-wise. He wouldn't even turn in my direction as I sat behind him.

But I was not to be beaten so easily. I went on whispering behind him, every now and then: 'Five hundred . . . Five hundred fifty. . . Five seventy-five. . . Six hundred. . .'

I added from time to time: 'You needn't bother about that mortgage. Fancy! Imagine! You can be absolutely free from it.' This was my running commentary in a subdued voice along with his music. When the bid came to eight hundred and fifty, he paused to ask in an undertone: 'What's the exact amount of that mortgage—do you remember?'

'One thousand two hundred. . .'

'Will they leave me alone when it is paid?'

'Yes—for a considerable time. . .'

'Do you guarantee my wife will not bother me about it any more?'

'Yes.'

'Then make it 1,200 and I will sing *mangalam* this very second.'

'Oh, that's too much, three times the fee . . .'

'Too much? I don't think so. You think music is a market commodity like tamarind to be bought with money. And so why should I not go the whole length with you?'

After this delivery, he cleared his throat and broke into a short *alapana* in *Yedukula Kambodhi*. His admirers, including the bridegroom, swayed as if hypnotized. I jumped down from the dais and went in to report to Balram. He gnashed his teeth and said: 'Let him sing till he falls dead but I'll not pay him a pie more.'

'Shall I cry "Fire! Fire!" or do some such thing?'

He thought over it and said: 'No. It would be inauspicious.'

At two a.m. the musician was offered a thousand rupees.

'Not less than twelve hundred,' he replied. 'I will stop it this very second.' In about half-an-hour, in the middle of a masterpiece in *Kapi*, I was able to negotiate the amount and offer it.

'You can stop now,' I said.

'Where is the amount?' he asked.

'Well that's to be presented on a plate at the end with due honours . . . I began.

'Not at all necessary,' he said. All this talk was carried on in an undertone accompanying the music; he even uttered many of his remarks in a musical manner—in the *raga* in which he was singing, so that others had no idea what was happening before their very eyes. With all the respect due to him, I felt like wringing his neck from behind. I thought if payment was delayed, a further rise in price might occur or the accompanists might take the cue and start some agitation of their own. I ran out and brought the cash. As he sang the glory of Krishna's life, an *Asthapadi*, I counted twelve one hundred rupee notes into his lap.

Balram never went near music again. He always says: 'Well, sir, it's not for us businessmen. We know nothing about it. We shall leave it alone. I wonder how *Sabha* secretaries manage these things. It must be a tough job.'

A Breach of Promise

Sankar was candidate 3,131 in the Lower Secondary Examination and he clearly saw this number on a typed sheet, announcing the results, pasted on the weather-beaten doors of the Government Middle School. That meant he would pass on to a High School now. He was slightly dizzy with joy.

He shuddered at the recollection of the same scene the year before when he had looked at the notices and found his number missing. He had thought he would never survive the failure and sit for another examination. Two of his closest friends had also passed this year, having failed with him the previous year. For them life had now acquired a new richness. There was a ring of joy in their voices and overflowing good-fellowship in every word they uttered to each other.

Sankar invited his friends to share with him a happy evening and went home to announce his success. He dinned the happy news into the ears of every person in the house, from his father down to the cook. He demanded from his mother five rupees as a reward for passing the examination, and went out.

He joined his friends. Their success was celebrated in a fitting manner. They first went to a restaurant, dragged chairs noisily about, thumped and roared and guffawed, and ate everything that the waiter suggested. They stayed in the restaurant till about six and then went to the Gaiety House, which was presenting to the public of Mysore the masterpiece *Blue and Black*. Sankar and his friends sat in the four-anna seats. When Georgie Lomb knitted his brow and said huskily to Vivian Troilet, 'Three years ago you did not want me; now I don't want you,' the boys nodded approvingly, but it was more from habit than from a full appreciation of Georgie Lomb's talent. For even Georgie Lomb occupied only a secondary place to the Lower Secondary results. The glow of success made the lights of ordinary life a little dim.

Next morning they met at four and started for the temple on the hill. It was by the grace of Goddess Chamundi that they had passed the examination and they must take offerings to her.

It was still dark when they reached the foot of the hill. All talk gradually ceased and their breathing became audible as they reached the two-hundredth step. They sat down for a while gazing at the twinkling lights of the city below. They rested till their breath came at more reasonable intervals and less noisily. Foot by foot they dragged themselves up the thousand steps—rugged granite steps which had acquired smoothness with the tread of a million pilgrims. They reached the top. An old woman sitting behind a heap of coconuts beckoned to them, 'Masters, won't you buy some offerings for the Goddess?' They stopped before her and bought coconuts, plantains, flowers and incense.

They entered the temple and circled the corridor thrice. A priest wrapped in a green shawl held a plate before them and they placed their offerings on it. They followed the priest into the shrine. He broke the coconuts at the altar, lighted the camphor and held up the flame before the image of the Goddess.

The diamonds on the image sparkled in the camphor light. Sankar and his friends closed their eyes and murmured, 'Mother, we have passed our examination through your grace. Bless us with success in all examinations hereafter.' The priest brought them the camphor flame on a plate; they touched it. They then received the holy water and the vermilion. Their coconuts and plantains, after they had been offered to the Goddess, were returned to them.

They went to the pillared hall outside and fell full-length on the floor before the Goddess. It was at this moment that a dreadful memory returned to Sankar's mind: the previous year on the evening before the examination he had come to the temple and prayed for success. He had prostrated himself before the Goddess and vowed secretly that if she made him fail in the examination he would destroy himself. He did fail that year, was miserable for some time, and passed the examination this year. He might possibly have remembered his vow if two of his best friends had not failed with him, if he had not gone away, after the results, to his sister's place for a month or two and spent a most exhilarating holiday there, and if he had not passed this year. Now as he lay before the Goddess he suddenly remembered his vow.

He rose and left the temple with his friends. His soul was troubled. A vow to God was a vow. Goddess Chamundi was not a mere idol but a living presence in the city. Did she not trample the evil demon Mahisha under her foot and tear his entrails out when he (as Sankar thought) defied her? Wherever one went in the city one saw pictures of this Goddess, with her hair untied and her hands blood-covered, driving a spear into the body of the demon under her foot. She was not a Goddess to be trifled with.

The next thing to do was to enjoy the plantains and the coconuts they had offered to the Goddess. They repaired to a secluded spot on the hill, shelled the coconuts and peeled the plantains. Sankar received his share, laid it beside him, and suddenly got up, saying, 'I shall go and get some jaggery. We cannot eat plain coconut.'

He ran towards the temple and entered the First Portal. No one was about, and he hopped on to a stone platform on the right side of the portal and slipped into a cave-like room. It was the entrance to the tower of the temple. The tower, visible for miles around, started as the broad gate of the temple, and going up, pile on pile, ended in an immense carved monster with a red lolling tongue and bulging eyes.

Sankar climbed an ancient ladder and reached a narrow room above. There was another ladder there and it led on to another room above. There were ten flights of ladders, the rooms becoming narrower and darker at every stage.

Sankar reached the topmost room. It was stifling and musty. Bats whirred about. A narrow beam of light came in through an aperture in the wall. He put his body through the aperture, rested his feet on some figures carved in relief on the outside of the tower, and reached the monster on top. Its eyes were as big as his head. He could lie curled up in its mouth. Its red, lolling tongue was like a platform. Sankar sat on it. The world below him was a splash of sunlight. The plains, over a thousand feet below, looked like patches of grass. He looked down and said to himself that he would be unrecognizable when he reached the ground. . . He closed his eyes and prayed, 'Great Mother, now I shall jump off from here and thus fulfil my vow. Forgive me for the delay.' He suspended his prayer, disturbed by a violent smarting at the elbow. He touched it. There was blood. Somewhere, probably while heaving himself up, he had skinned his elbow. It was raw. Blood was oozing. It smarted. He groaned. He prayed, 'Great Mother, you must forgive me. I cannot throw myself down. Instead, for a year I will come here every Friday and offer two coconuts.' He rose very carefully, held his breath, and climbed down, resting his feet on carved images. His legs trembled. A look below made his head reel. He reached the aperture, slid through it into the top room, and sat down for a moment and closed his eyes.

The moment Sankar appeared, his friends cursed him for taking such a long time to return and demanded, 'Where is the jaggery?' Sankar turned round without a word and ran at full speed towards the shop before the temple where jaggery was sold.

The Magic Beard

The Talkative Man said:

'I tried to do one thing after another for a living and failed miserably. I grew tired of everything and started massaging my chin with coconut oil every morning. How could coconut-oil-massage be a remedy for unemployment? I'll tell you how. I met a wise old man who commanded me to take a vow not to shave or cut my hair till I found some means of earning money. An easy enough vow. I was ordinarily blessed with a rapid growth on my scalp and face, and now I facilitated nature with coconut-oil-massage.

'When I came down to Madras a few days later I looked like a mystic. A magnificent beard and moustache covered my face and I had long hair streaming down to my shoulders. I could not see myself in a mirror without feeling a sort of reverence for my face. But this imposing appearance did not carry me far. I tramped up and down the city and saw numerous people, but all to no purpose. The utmost my beard achieved for me was that people received me respectfully, and uttered their refusals in an apologetic tone.

'One afternoon I was standing on the kerb in front of the Law College. I had a heavy heart and sore feet, and stood vacantly staring at the callous, indifferent humanity going up and down in their trams, buses and motor cars. An old woman stood before me and held out her hand for a coin. "Get away!" I said as usual. I had my last three pies in my purse and I was irritated that an old woman should come and claim even that. I bared my teeth and cursed her. She became indignant: "You may have no money, but kind words cost nothing. Would you have behaved in this manner if your mother had come and asked for money?" This touched a raw corner in my heart. I remembered the scowls I put on and the cynicisms I poured out whenever my mother asked me for money. I particularly remembered how I made her return to the hawker a small aluminium vessel, costing a few annas, which she had bought for the house. After her death this remained a harrowing memory with me: the childlike enthusiasm with which she took the vessel and the utter disappointment with which she returned it.

Now this old woman had started this memory all over again. "This is my only coin, take it," I said, giving her the three pies. She took it and went away. I moved to the edge of the pavement and supported myself against the railing. I really didn't know what to do with myself. The old woman came back in a quarter-of-an-hour. She panted with joy as she held up a four-anna silver coin and said, "God bless you, sir. Yours is a lucky hand. I did not earn a single pie since the morning but the moment you gave me money a lot of others, too, are giving me money. Someone has given me a four-anna piece. Four annas! There are certain great souls whose slightest touch opens a treasure. You are one such."

"'If my touch is so precious don't you think I ought to be paid for it?"

"'Surely, master. Here you are." She gave me an anna. An anna represented a great many things for me in life: a cup of coffee, a tram ticket, and, who could say, if my latest idea should prove practicable, four copper pieces of luck, and at least four annas from beggars. I walked down China Bazaar Road. An old man accosted me. "Look here, old man," I said, "I have a lucky hand. If I give you a coin it will soon multiply. If it happens what will you give me?"

"'A quarter of what I earn, master."

'I gave him a copper coin and sent him out. He returned half-an-hour later, his face beaming with joy. "There is surely some magic in your touch, master. I had only to hold out my hand and coins fell on it. I don't know what has come over everybody. They have only to see my hand and they drop coins in it. Even people sitting in cars, people who usually get their drivers to chase me away, have given me money today!" He gave me an anna-and-a-half.

'Next day I was back in George Town and hit off a bargain with every decent beggar I met. At the Law College kerb I met the old woman. I gave her a coin and in a short while she returned and gave me nearly four annas. And then I moved down and met the old man. I earned a couple of annas from him. I took the tram for Mount Road and earned nearly eight annas from a one-legged urchin, a little girl with six fingers, and a woman carrying twins.

'I felt that this surely deserved to be placed on a business footing with proper organization.

'In a few days I had an office in George Town. At first I squatted on a gutter-lid in China Bazaar Road to sell my wares, that is luck, like the rest of them there selling cuff-links, moth-balls, toys, sweets and piece-goods; but I soon found that it was rather awkward to be transacting business with my staff of beggars in a public place. I had to seek seclusion. The shade of a tree behind the High Court seemed ideal for this. There were a lot of people there, no doubt, but they were all so wrapped up in their own troubles that they did not take any notice of me.

'With the help of the old woman I selected about ten beggars. I strictly avoided blind beggars and beggars with infectious diseases. My staff consisted of a stalwart who swathed his body in bandages and walked on crutches though his limbs were sound: he stood before a large coffee hotel and whined the whole day; a "blind" boy who was blind in only one eye though he shut both his eyes and sent forth pitiful cries the whole day at every bus-stand; an old man whose limbs were paralyzed; the old woman; and so on.

'I met them punctually at ten o'clock in the morning behind the High Court, and gave them each a coin. They went away and returned at midday. I checked their collections and took my fee. They went out again after an hour's rest and met me at five o'clock.

'Through my lucky touch everyone had doubled his income. The stalwart in bandages had not been making more than ten annas before; now his income never went below a rupee-and-a-half, which meant that I got at least six annas from him. The old woman earned about a rupee now; the "blind" boy brought in a rupee and four annas. My total income was about three rupees a day now. Ninety rupees a month!

'On the first of the next month I sent a money order for fifty rupees to my wife. She was elated and asked what I was doing. I merely replied that I helped people to make money and collected a little commission for the service. She asked why I should not be making all that money myself!

'I looked at beggars, when I came out of a cinema or at the beach, with a professional eye, and was racked with the feeling that a vast army of them was simply going to waste. I soon realized that I could make more money with a little wider organization.

'Shortly, I established three more centres: one under a tree in the People's Park, to cover the Moore Market, the Central Station, and the General Hospital Road. I had another in Mount Road with the office in the porch of an old shop and a third one in Puraswalkam with the office on the tank bund. Later I opened a one-hour office at the beach in the porch of the Revenue Board Office. In any case I spent my evenings there and I thought I might combine relaxation with a little business.

'I arranged my timetable efficiently, and visited all the centres in the course of the day. I had a monthly tram pass and over and above it I spent ten rupees a month on bus journeys.

'On the first of the next month I sent home two hundred rupees. My wife was tremendously pleased. She wrote suggesting a number of things I might buy for her. She incidentally asked if I had had a clean shave and a haircut. She was quite right. Why should I still wear the frightful jungle on my face and head? My vow was fulfilled, I was earning money.

'That afternoon I went to a shaving saloon and came out of it with a smooth face and a very close crop. Gone was the mystic. It was very refreshing when the wind blew on my face unhindered. I caught a glimpse of myself in a shop mirror on the way and thought it was someone else. I also felt a little ashamed of my face. There is something foolish in a man's smooth appearance when his old beard and moustache are suddenly shaved off.

'When I sat down under the tree behind the High Court that afternoon, my friends came and passed me indifferently.

'"Where are you fellows going?" I asked.

'"We are beggars, master. Please give us a coin."

'"Idiots! Don't you recognize me?"

'"No, sir."

'"Is my voice not familiar?"

'"Yes, sir, but how can we know who you are?"

'They wouldn't believe me when I told them who I was.

'I argued with them for half-an-hour. They treated me as an impostor. I grew angry and desperate. I told the old woman finally, "I will give you a coin with my hand. If it brings you more coins will you believe who I am?"

'"Yes, sir." She went and returned in about twenty minutes. Her lips were twitching with anger and grief. She said, "You are not our master. She would be a wretched woman who accepted a coin from your hand. If my master had given me the coin with his hand, coins would have come rushing in to join it. But now? People wrenched my hand and swore at me; and in that shop over there they were so violent that I lost my temper, and a man came to beat me, and in the scuffle I lost even the few coins I had collected in the morning."

'They walked away in great rage. I sat under the tree and watched them go, rubbing my smooth chin with my fingers.

'The same thing happened at every centre that day. I couldn't collect a pie. I was amazed that a little change in appearance should affect people so much. And every time I tried to establish my identity with a lucky coin, the person who carried it lost all the money he had and was even beaten.'

Around a Temple

The Talkative Man said:

'Some years ago we had a forestry officer in this town who scoffed at things. He was sent down by his department for some special work in Mempi Forest and he had his headquarters here. You know the kind of person. He had spent a couple of years abroad, and after returning home he was full of contempt for all our practices and institutions. He was strictly "rational" by which he meant that he believed only in things he could touch, see, hear and smell. God didn't pass any of these tests, at any rate the God we believed in. Accordingly to most of us, God resides in the Anjaneya temple we see on the way.

'It is a very small temple, no doubt, but it is very ancient. It is right at the centre of the town, at the cutting of the two most important roads— Lawley Road running east and west and the Trunk Road running north and south; and any person going out anywhere, whether to the court or the college, the market or the Extension, has to pass the temple. And no one is so foolish as to ignore the God and carry on. He is very real and He can make His power felt. I do not say that He showers good fortune on those who bow to Him; I do not mean that at all. But I do mean that it is very simple to please a god. It costs about a quarter-of-an-anna a week and five minutes of prayer on a Saturday evening. Ninety-nine out of a hundred do it and are none the worse for it. On any Saturday evening you can see a thousand people at the temple, going round the image and burning camphor.

'I have said that the temple is at an important crossing, and every time our friend passed up and down either to his office or club he had to pass it, and you may be sure, particularly on Saturday evenings, the crowd around the temple caused dislocation of traffic. Lesser beings faced it cheerfully. But our friend was always annoyed. He would remark to his driver: "Run over the blasted crowd. Superstitious mugs. If this town had a sane municipality this temple would have been pulled down years ago . . ."

'On a Sunday morning the driver asked: "May I have the afternoon off, sir?"

'"Why?"

'"When my child fell ill some days ago I vowed I would visit the cross-road shrine with my family. . ."

'"Today?"

'"Yes, sir. On other days it is crowded."

'"You can't go today."

'"I have to, sir. It is a duty. . ."

'"You can't go. You can't have leave for all your superstitious humbug-ging." The driver was so insistent that the officer told him a few minutes later: "All right, go. Come on the first of next month and take your pay. You are dismissed."

'At five o'clock when he started for his club he felt irritated. He had no driver. "I will do without these fellows," he said to himself. "Why should I depend upon anyone?"

'The chief reason why he depended upon others was that he was too nervous to handle a car. His head was a whirl of confusion when he sat at the wheel. He had not driven more than fifty miles in all his life though he had a driving licence and renewed it punctually every year. Now as he thought of the race of chauffeurs he felt bitter: "I will teach these beggars a lesson. Drivers aren't heaven-born. Just ordinary fellows. It is all a question of practice; one has to make a beginning somewhere. I will teach these superstitious beggars a lesson. India will never become a first-rate nation as long as it worships traffic-obstructing gods, which any sensible municipality ought to remove."

'It was years since he had driven a car. With trepidation he opened the garage door and climbed in. At a speed of about twenty-five miles an hour his car shot out of the gate after it had finally emerged from the throes of gear-changing. It flew past the temple and presently our friend realized that somehow he could not turn to his left, as he must, if he wanted to reach his club. He could only steer to his right. Nor could he stop the car when he wanted. He felt that applying the brakes was an extraordinarily queer business. When he tried to stop he committed so many blunders that the car rocked, danced and threatened to burst. He felt it safest to go up the road till a favourable opportunity presented itself for him to turn right, and then again right, and about-turn. He whizzed past the temple back to his bungalow, where he could not stop, and so had to proceed again, turn right, go up the Trunk Road, turn right again, and come down the road past the temple.

'Half-an-hour later the dismissed driver arrived at the shrine with his family and was nearly run over. He stepped aside and had hardly recovered from the shock when the car reappeared. The driver put away his basket of offerings, took his family to a place of safety, and came out. When the car appeared again he asked, "What is the matter, sir?" His master looked at him pathetically and before he could answer the car came round again: "Can't stop."

"'Use the hand-brake, sir, the foot-brake's rather loose."

"'I can't," panted our friend.

'The driver realized that the only thing his master could do with a car was to turn its wheel right and blow the horn. He asked, "Have you put in any petrol, sir?"

"'No."

"It had only one-and-a-half gallons; let it run it out." The driver went in, performed *puja*, sent away his family and attempted to jump on the footboard. He couldn't. He stood aside on a temple step with folded hands, patiently waiting for the car to exhaust its petrol.

'The car soon came to a stop. The gentleman gave a gasp and fainted on the steering wheel. He was revived. When he came to, the priest of the temple held before him a plate and said, "Sir, you have circled the temple over five hundred times today. Ordinarily people go round only nine times, and on special occasions one hundred-and-eight times. I haven't closed the doors thinking you might like to offer coconut and camphor at the end of your rounds." The officer flung a coin on the tray.

'The driver asked, "Can I be of any service, sir?"

"'Yes, drive the car home."

'He reinstated the driver, who demanded a raise a fortnight later. And whenever our friend passed the temple, he exercised great self-control and never let an impatient word cross his lips. I won't say that he became very devout all of a sudden, but he certainly checked his temper and tongue when he was in the vicinity of the temple. And wasn't it enough achievement for a god?'

The Magic Cure

Kannan was returning home to the village from the coconut garden, and as he came to the end of the narrow track through the fields he heard low moans in Thayi's cottage.

He pushed the door open and peeped inside. Thayi was on the floor writhing.

'What is wrong with you, old woman?' he asked.

After a prelude of moans Thayi replied: 'It is this wretched pain here.' She indicated her stomach. 'This is the worst attack that I have ever had.'

She moaned and writhed. Kannan tried to soothe her.

'Why don't you take some medicine, sister?' he asked.

'Medicine? I take everything that everybody suggests.'

'Why don't you go to the physician on the hills? They say he can cure even leprosy.'

'All doctors are swindlers. They give you coloured water and take away all your money.'

'Why don't you go to the Government doctors, who have read English?' suggested Kannan.

'English doctors! With their needles and knives and bitter pills! I would not go near them even if they offered me money.'

Kannan looked reflective, and said: 'You are right, sister. No physician can do you any good. The thing that is bothering you in the belly is not an ordinary stomachache. The devil has got in there. You are possessed.'

The old woman wailed on hearing this. 'Don't say so, brother.'

'What am I to do? I never speak untruth,' said Kannan.

The old woman sobbed at her fate. Kannan gave her the consolations of philosophy.

'What is the use of crying, old one?' he asked. 'Fate. Fate. No one can do anything.'

'It is the devil,' continued Kannan after a pause. 'He will start at the belly, slowly work upward, and crack your skull before he goes out.'

The old woman beat her stomach, swayed forward and backward, and cried.

'I had a niece in the next village,' said Kannan. 'She had been complaining of stomachache for a year or two, and then one day as she was working in the field she suddenly fell down, and before anyone could go to her help her skull burst. They say the noise of the explosion was heard beyond the Kali temple.'

The old woman sat sobbing.

'There is one hope for you,' said Kannan. 'There is a holy man in a village four stones from here. He can exorcise the worst devil. He is known to me.'

'Brother, bring him here,' said Thayi, gripping his arm.

'I will try. But I won't promise.'

Three days later Kannan came to tell her he had come to know that the holy man would be passing that way and he would try to bring him to her house on Friday.

On Friday morning, Thayi got up at four o'clock, scrubbed the floor of her cottage, washed all the vessels and pots, and draped the front doorway with a festoon of mango leaves. She bought coconuts, betel leaves, plantains, incense sticks, camphor, and a heap of yellow flowers. She placed the flowers, coconut and betel leaves on mud trays in the middle of the floor, and spread her best mat before them. Then she lighted the incense sticks.

At about midday Kannan and the holy man arrived. The sight of the holy man, with his ash-smeared face and flaming eyes, filled Thayi with awe. He had three rows of a rosary around his neck.

They sat on the mat, and Thayi sat before them.

The holy man asked for a mud pot and decked it with the yellow flowers. He placed lighted wicks before it, and circled the incense sticks over it. He uttered some strange incantations in a deep, booming voice.

Then he suddenly picked up a cane, rapped Thayi on the back, and boomed: 'Will you go now?'

Thayi did not know what to say. The cane descended on her again, and the question was repeated more ferociously than before. When the cane came down a third time Kannan said 'Say yes.'

The old woman said 'Yes'.

'It was the devil who answered yes,' interpreted Kannan.

The holy man sat with closed eyes, and asked suddenly: 'Where are the jewels?'

'Alas, I have no jewels,' said Thayi.

'Liar,' said Kannan. 'We are not going to run away with your jewels. He wants them just for a moment. Without the jewels nothing can be done.'

'Forgive me, masters,' said the old woman, and dug up a small box from the belly of a grain pot. It contained jewels for a future daughter-in-law, when the old woman's son should return from the town, marry, and settle down in the village.

'Put the jewels in the pot,' commanded the holy man. Thayi took out of the box two silver anklets, two silver bangles, some ear ornaments, a silver ring, and a bead necklace, and deposited them carefully in the bottom of the flower-decked pot.

The holy man gave her a final thwack with the cane, saying 'Begone!' and put the lid on the pot. He then took an incense stick held it over the pot, and gave it to the old woman. He told her to take the incense stick to a far corner of the backyard, and plant it in the ground.

When Thayi returned from the backyard she found the pot sealed with a cloth tied over the lid and knotted tightly.

The holy man said: 'Now your pain is gone, old woman. You are free from the devil now. Don't open this pot for three months. The devil who tormented you is in it, lured by the jewels. It will be dead in three months and not before. If you open the pot before the devil is dead it will tear you to shreds. Take care!'

A fortnight later Kannan was going round the coconut garden, marking the trees which were affected by pests. He felt drowsy in the green glare of the afternoon. He was just wondering why he should not unwind his turban, spread it under a tree, and sleep for a while, when he heard the creaking of sandals behind him. He saw Bheema, the village constable, coming towards him.

'Ah, you are welcome to my garden, brother,' said Kannan.

'I hope I see you well,' said the constable.

'Yes, by God's mercy, I am well.'

'I am glad to hear that. Will you come with me now?'

'Where to?'

'Our Inspector wants to see you. He has bought some coconut seedlings and he wants you to help plant them.'

'I will certainly come,' said Kannan. 'Would you like some coconut juice?'

Bheema considered the offer. He was thirsty, and coconut juice would be ideal now. But to get it, the other would have to be sent up a tree, and suppose he stayed there? Bheema himself could not climb a tree even if a tiger was behind him.

'No, brother,' said Bheema. 'My throat is sore, and they say coconut juice is bad for the throat.'

As he passed the jasmine arch over the rickety gates of the village police station Kannan felt nervous. The Inspector was sitting at a table. On seeing Kannan he left the table, approached him, and slapped him in the face.

After this preparation the Inspector asked: 'Where are old Thayi's jewels, you heir of a swindler?'

Kannan burst into tears. At the end of twenty minutes, after he had been reduced to a squirming, half-dead jelly, Kannan opened his mouth.

'Stop. Don't kick me, please. I will speak the truth. The jewels are with a pawnbroker in the town. They were worth thirty-six rupees, and he gave us eighteen rupees; and we took nine rupees each. The other is my brother-in-law and lives in a village four stones from here. I have spoken the truth. Don't kill me. . .'

The Sub-magistrate sentenced Kannan and the 'holy man' to six months' rigorous imprisonment. The jewels were restored to the old woman.

As he gave her the jewels the Inspector said: 'Go home. May God keep you out of the hands of scoundrels. You really owe your jewels to your stomachache. If you had not got the attack again you would not have suspected, and if you had not suspected you would not have opened the mud pot for three months; and anything might have happened in three months, you know.'

'I agree with you, master. You are learned and wise.'

That evening Thayi went to the temple of Hanuman. She broke a coconut, lighted a piece of camphor before the God, and whispered fervently: 'My father, I am grateful to you for the stomachache you have given me.'

The Image

The following story is based upon the traditional accounts of the life of the famous sculptor, Jakanachari, who built the Belur, Halebid and other Hoysala temples, in the reign of Vishnuvardhana (AD12th century). For the purposes of the story a few deviations from the accepted accounts are included.

The temple of Belur was nearly ready. At the next full moon it was to be consecrated and opened for worship. The old sculptor, Jakanachari, was working on the main image of the temple in the inner shrine. He spoke to no one and tolerated no interruption. As he was working he noticed a shadow falling on the wall. He had ordered that no one was to be allowed to disturb him. He turned sharply with a curse on his lip, but he swallowed the curse quickly, fell down and touched the floor with his forehead. The king had come in noiselessly.

'You go on with your work,' said the king.

'I obey,' said the sculptor. He was working on the drapery of the image. The king watched the image, fascinated, as godliness grew upon it with each stroke: there was grace in its eyes and protection in its gesture.

The king said, 'Jakanacharya, I am longing for the day when I may offer worship to this Kesava. When will you finish your work?'

'Sire, by God's grace, I hope to finish the work by full moon.'

When the king left, the old sculptor, plying his delicate chisel, conjured up a vision of the day of consecration. At the auspicious moment while priests chanted and smoke curled up from the sacred fire, he would place the god on his pedestal. He could almost hear now the babble of voices. And the king stood on the threshold of the shrine with the minister beside him, having arrived in state on his elephant; people from all over the empire were crowding in for the occasion. As the image was fixed to its pedestal, a great cry of joy went up from the crowd, and the king presented the sculptor with a gold bracelet.

Jakanachari did not break off for food at noon. In the ecstasy of the vision he forgot hunger. Someone had the kindness to remind him. He merely replied, 'Get out and don't talk to me.' A little later he turned from the image and was annoyed to see someone standing at the doorway and watching the image.

'Go away,' said the sculptor.

'Yes, I will go away as soon as I have seen as much of the image as I like.'

'Oh, oh! Who may you be?'

'I am a wanderer. I happened to pass this way and dropped in to have a look at the temple.'

'Get away now or I will have you pushed out. No one must see this image before it is completed.'

'I am one interested in stone. I can do a little work myself.'

'Oh, you are a master, are you?'

'I don't say that. But ever since I can remember I have loved stones.'

'You are an upstart. Now let me see nothing more of you,' said the old man.

'Say what you like,' replied the stranger. 'I have gone round and seen all that is to be seen. The pillars are divine; the figures on the outer walls are the work of a godly hand. This temple will be remembered by coming generations as the greatest.'

'I do not need your certificate.'

'Hear me fully,' said the young man. 'I am not speaking now to flatter you. I am merely expressing a fact. I say once again that all that you have done so far is wonderful, except. . .'

Now the old sculptor pricked up his ears and cried, 'Except what? Except what?'

'Except the work you are now doing.'

The old man picked up his mallet and flourished it at the intruder.

'I will smash your skull if you speak any more.'

'At your age you must have greater self-possession,' said the young man. 'I am not saying that your work is bad but your choice of stone is unlucky.'

'Your words are inauspicious,' wailed the old man.

'With that stone you could make a figure for a gateway but not the main God of an inner shrine. After all, the tens and thousands of carvings and decorations are only a setting for the main image, and its stone should have the utmost purity. Now this stone has a flaw, and the image is unfit for worship and consecration.'

'Oh, will no one drag this man away! His words are inauspicious.'

'I am merely warning you with the best of motives. Don't get angry. I repeat that this stone has a flaw, and I am surprised that a man of your experience did not notice it.'

'Young fool, you don't know what you are saying. See this arm: it has chipped and carved fifty thousand forms of God, but I swear I will cut this off if you prove what you are saying.'

The stranger replied, 'Don't say such serious things. I merely said something about the stone because I thought you might like to hear it. Take it for what it is worth. Don't do such a terrible thing.'

'No, you shall prove it.'

'I will prove it but not if you are going to cut off your arm. I will even say where the flaw is.'

'Where?'

'Around the navel of the image.'

'Young man, I will tell the king and have you put in chains if you don't get out this moment.'

'All right, I will go,' said the young man and turned to go. While crossing the courtyard he turned round and shouted, 'I am going, but bear in mind my warning.'

The old man ran after him, gripped his arm, and said, 'Stop now, I will not let you go.' He yelled for everyone in the place. A crowd gathered. He told the crowd: 'This young fool holds that Kesava is made of a stone which has a flaw. If he proves it I will cut off my right arm. If he does not I will cut off his arm and make him ride out on a donkey.'

The stranger said, 'I refuse to prove anything. Now let me go.'

The old sculptor held him by the arm and said, 'Either you prove what you have said or I will chop off your arm and haul you up on a donkey, though if I tell the king he will chop off your head.'

'All right,' said the stranger, 'I accept the challenge. Don't blame me afterwards. Will someone bring me a little paste of sandalwood?'

It was brought.

He said, 'May I go near the image?'

'Yes, you may.'

The young man walked into the shrine with the sculptor, the crowd following them. The image stood leaning against a block of stone, looking on all this scene of strife with an unruffled calm. The stranger asked, 'May I touch it?'

'No,' said the old man. 'What do you want to do?'

'I want this sandal paste to be smeared over the image from the chest down. Will you do it?' The old man smeared the sandal paste as he was directed.

'Now watch it,' said the stranger. The paste dried quickly and stood out in whitish flakes.

'What has it proved?' asked the crowd derisively.

'Has the sandal paste dried all over?' asked the young man.

'Yes.'

'See near the navel of the image,' said the young man; and where he pointed there was a wet patch the circumference of a little coin.

'It is still wet,' said someone.

'Do you want to watch till it dries up?'

'Yes.'

'Then you may spend the rest of your life watching it, but it won't dry, because underneath it there is a cavity with water, and in that water there may be a toad living.'

The sculptor said grimly, 'I have never allowed anyone to touch my implements but I am about to break that habit now because I may have no more use for them henceforth. Here, take my mallet and chisel and break that navel and show me what is inside.'

The young man was at first reluctant to break the idol, but the sculptor was insistent. The young man held the chisel and with a deft stroke hit out a circular flake at the navel. A little water flowed out, and out peeped a very baffled toad.

The sculptor said, 'My career is now over. I wish I had never been born.' In that crowd there was a guard with a sword in his belt. The old man snatched it off. 'Now I fulfil my vow, and gladly do it. I have no use for this arm.'

The young stranger wrenched his wrist till he dropped the sword. 'You will not do it. When I came here it was to see all this work and learn whatever there was to be learnt. I did not come here to deprive you of your arm. Now I will be going.' He appealed to those around him: 'Please see that he does no violence to himself.' He added, 'My purpose was only to prevent the consecration and worship of a toad. Please watch this old man.' He turned to go.

Jakanachari called him and said, 'I admire your feeling for stone. God bless you. Where do you come from?'

'My home is in Kridapura,' said the stranger.

'Kridapura!' repeated the old man and became reflective. 'Kridapura! Who are you? Who is your father?'

'I don't know. I am in search of him,' said the stranger.

'Oh tell me more about yourself,' said Jakanachari.

The stranger said, 'When I was yet unborn, that is a month before I was born, my father left home one evening and never returned.'

'What was his name?'

'Krishna Deva,' replied the stranger.

The sculptor said, 'Listen now. I will tell you something I know. It was very good of your mother to send you out to search for the old absconder, considering the manner in which he left. But this is to be said for him. He had a life of dedication before him, a life in the service of God. He saw it in a vision. The choice was between family attachments and utter dedication. There was no middle way; and he made his choice abruptly and uncompromisingly, the only way in which any choice in life can be made. And he never looked back with regret because gods above and kings below have been kind.'

'You know so much about him!' said the stranger.

'Yes, because Krishna Deva concealed himself behind a new name: Jakanachari.'

An hour later he said, 'My son, now take me home. My career is over. I may not cut off my arm, but I will never again touch my chisel and mallet. When my eyes and hands cannot discriminate between stone and stone, it is time to put down the chisel and wait for death.'

The sculptor returned to Kridapura. With all the comfort he could derive from regaining home and family he was secretly very unhappy. For he was essentially a creature who throve on his art. And the self-imposed separation from his work was agonizing. He would have withered away and died of this want like a plant kept away from sunlight but for a dream he had a few months after his return: he was commanded to build a temple in Kridapura and dedicate it to Kesava. He obeyed this command and built the temple, and a number of others along with it. After this the name of the place was changed from Kridapura to Kai Dala, which means: The Restored Arm.

Today Kai Dala is an obscure little village, a few miles off Tumkur. It is known to have been the capital of a state at one time. Nothing of that ancient glory is now left, except the temple with its magnificent Kesava, which stands even today to commemorate the resurrection of an artist.

MORE ABOUT PENGUINS

For further information about books available from Penguins in India write to Penguin Books (India) Ltd, B4/246, Safdarjung Enclave, New Delhi 110 029.

In the UK: For a complete list of books available from Penguins in the United Kingdom write to Dept. EP, Penguin Books Ltd, Harmondsworth, Middlesex UB7 0DA.

In the U.S.A.: For a complete list of books available from Penguins in the United States write to Dept. DG, Penguin Books, 299 Murray Hill Parkway, East Rutherford, New Jersey 07073.

In Canada: For a complete list of books available from Penguins in Canada write to Penguin Books Canada Ltd, 2801 John Street, Markham, Ontario L3R 1B4.

In Australia: For a complete list of books available from Penguins in Australia write to the Marketing Department, Penguin Books Australia Ltd, P.O. Box 257, Ringwood, Victoria 3134.

In New Zealand: For a complete list of books available from Penguins in New Zealand write to the Marketing Department, Penguin Books (N.Z.) Ltd, Private Bag, Takapuna, Auckland 9.

A WRITER'S NIGHTMARE
R.K. Narayan

R.K. Narayan, perhaps India's best-known living writer, is better known as a novelist but his essays are as delightful and enchanting as his stories and novels. *A Writer's Nightmare* includes essays on subjects as diverse as weddings, higher mathematics, South Indian coffee, umbrellas, monkeys, the caste system—all sorts of topics, simple and not so simple, which reveal the very essence of India.

'(A book) to be dipped into and savoured'
— *Sunday*

FOR THE BEST IN PAPERBACKS, LOOK FOR THE 🐧

MY DATELESS DIARY
R.K. Narayan

At the age of fifty, R.K. Narayan, who already enjoyed a fair amount of success abroad, left his country for the first time and landed smack in the middle of the frenetic turmoil of New York City. In this wonderfully funny and crisply observed travelogue, Narayan, arguably India's greatest living writer, gives us his view of the United States of America.

"Witty and often hilarious... view of the U.S." —*Sunday Herald*

THE HOTEL RIVIERA
R.K. Laxman

The arrival of Sabitha, a voluptuous and sensual 'orphan' at the Hotel Riviera, a squalid little flophouse in Bombay, destroys forever the amicable co-existence of its inhabitants.

For a start, Sabitha's presence has a cataclysmic effect on the manager of the hotel, an inhibited small-town person, who is totally unmanned by the glamorous vamp. Madly in love, he begins to come apart mentally and physically when she rejects all his amorous overtures. As the path of true love becomes increasingly rocky, the manager turns morose and hostile towards the other employees and long-term residents of the hotel—Rao, the clerk, a relative of the proprietor, **Achar**, the cook who believes in spoon-down strikes at the least word of criticism, Francis, the liftman and resident snoop, the Major, a gun-waving, alcoholic hotel guest, **Swamiji**, an amazingly incompetent godman and several others—and they in turn gang up against him. Frantic, the manager tries to resolve all his problems at one stroke but only succeeds in adding more chaos to an already hilariously confused situation.

"Laxman's novel is inhabited by ordinary people trapped in ordinary situations, seeking escape-routes into a world more exciting than the one available."
—*Indian Express*